REAP THE WHIRLWIND

Briana, passionate about environmental protection, is visiting Turtle Island in the Caribbean. When she discovers Phoebe, the elderly owner of the island, is considering selling it to Nick, Briana is concerned that he'd exploit the island. Determined to prevent this, she attempts to establish 'friendly tourism' there instead, although Nick is extremely sceptical. In reality he doesn't want to change a thing — but certainly relishes a fight. But when Phoebe has a heart attack, he blames Briana's new scheme . . .

WENDY KREMER

REAP THE WHIRLWIND *J*

Complete and Unabridged

LINFORD
Leicester

First published in Great Britain in 2008

First Linford Edition
published 2010

British Library CIP Data

Kremer, Wendy.
   Reap the whirlwind.- -
   (Linford romance library)
   1. Sustainable tourism- -Fiction.
   2. Islands- -Caribbean Area- -Fiction.
   3. Love stories.
   4. Large type books.
   I. Title II. Series
   823.9′2–dc22

   ISBN 978-1-44480-111-8

Published by
F. A. Thorpe (Publishing)
Anstey, Leicestershire

Set by Words & Graphics Ltd.
Anstey, Leicestershire
Printed and bound in Great Britain by
T. J. International Ltd., Padstow, Cornwall

This book is printed on acid-free paper

1

Peering into the declining sunset, Phoebe McAllister watched silently as the yacht mastered its passage through the outer reef. Her voice echoed her pleasure. 'It's Nick!' Her wrinkled face turned briefly to Briana. 'You know who I mean, don't you? Nick . . . Nicolas Thornton!'

Briana tried to recall references to a *Nick* in Phoebe's letters to her grandmother. She shook her head. 'No.'

'An old friend . . . he's been coming here ever since he could sail a boat.'

'Oh, I see.'

Phoebe laughed gruffly. 'He comes regularly, even though I tell him to invest his time more profitably elsewhere . . . but from what I gather he's never short of female company, so . . . ' She shrugged and stopped in mid-stream to follow the yacht's progress until it was safe within the lagoon. The anchor hit the water with an audible splash, and they watched him moving around the deck.

The yacht was bobbing up and down on the sun-tipped waves of the lagoon as he lowered a dinghy and climbed down to it with practised ease. Looking up briefly at pale clouds that were fringed with luminous red against a gold and crimson sky, he touched the peak of his cap and took hold of the oars. Directing the small craft with powerful strokes towards the beach, his voice drifted across the water when he spotted them. A welcoming committee? 'Hi, Phoebe!' Speeding across the dark green waters, he rapidly covered the distance to the beach.

The light was fading fast now, but Briana was still able to make out his face as he drew nearer. His features were chiselled — almost gaunt. There was a purposeful thrust to his chin, and the shadow of a beard gave him a rugged, almost piratical appearance. She told herself to stop fantasising; this Caribbean air was making her light-headed.

They waited patiently for him to beach the dinghy. His canvas shoes left large imprints on the wet coral sand as he strode towards them; a small package wedged under his arm.

He enveloped Phoebe in a swift hug, sweeping her off her feet and she made a belated effort to protest. 'One of these days you'll break my ribs.' He set her down on the sand, and she attempted to look annoyed.

'Never! You're as strong as an old donkey. Here! Your favourites!' He placed the small plywood box in her hands, and tipped his chin in Briana's direction. 'Your visitor from the UK?'

Briana pulled some stray hair out of her eyes with the tips of her fingers, and stared up into his face. He had dark brown eyes and thick black hair that tapered neatly to his collar. His black eyebrows lifted, and a smile softened his features as he noted with approval the shoulder-length tresses, shapely thighs and long legs. His glance slid casually over her, as sea breezes plastered the flimsy material of her dress to her body.

Phoebe laughed. 'I resent the old donkey bit — but thanks for these!' Phoebe waved the box in the air.

Briana noticed the word *cheroots* splashed across the lid.

'Oh! This is Briana, Briana Norton! You've heard me talk about her often enough. Briana, this is Nick!'

Briana threw back her shoulders and thrust out her hand. 'Hello! Pleased to meet you.'

He touched the peak of his hat, gave her a friendly nod, and his hand met hers in a warm clasp. 'The pleasure's all mine, I'm sure!'

Phoebe's voice cut through their meeting. 'Supper is almost ready. I suppose you want to join us?'

He responded matter-of-factly. 'I heard about your visitor, and thought there might be a good meal to be had this evening.'

Phoebe laughed gruffly. 'Trust you! It seems I can't have a visitor without the whole place gossiping. Windblown Island is sometimes like an oriental bazaar!' She peered at the large practical watch on her bony wrist, and straightened her body slowly.

Her back ached badly today, but that was one of the prices one paid for growing old — sometimes the brain and the body didn't dance to the same kind of music. 'Right. We may as well go home now! I wanted to show Briana the lagoon as the sun is going down, but we dawdled, and missed most of it.'

Addressing Briana, Nick Thornton said. 'Yes, the evening skies are fantastic. You never get used to all the colour — I'm still amazed, and I was born here.'

Briana nodded and groped around for an answer. She found him vaguely disturbing, her cheeks felt hot and she hoped he didn't notice her confusion. 'My grandmother brought back lots of photos, but I expect they don't do the island justice.'

'Photos are flat images; nothing compares to the real McCoy.' His eyes were intent, appraising. She held his glance and managed a weak smile. He was the kind of man that disturbed your peace of mind with his mere presence; he was attractive and had an air of authority.

Briana certainly hadn't come here looking for romance, and wasn't going to let her imagination run riot about a man she'd just met — she didn't know a thing about him, apart from the fact that Phoebe liked him.

The trail back to Phoebe's straggling house meandered through a tunnel of evergreen tropical vegetation. The path was well trodden and Briana's sandalled feet travelled over soft ground.

This small Caribbean island was paradise come true. Nature had been left to its own devices, and the island was still unexploited, mainly because

Phoebe had never been able to convince a bank that any of her ongoing schemes were feasible propositions.

Nothing had worked well, and through the years the population of Turtle Island dwindled. Although Briana felt sorry that Phoebe lacked any steady income (apart from some meagre interest she got from some small investments made in her father's lifetime), Briana was still glad that Turtle Island had avoided the so-called blessing of civilisation. Briana's involvement in environmental protection had honed her attitude, and made her aware of how commercialism brutally destroyed places, and ruined people's lives, just for financial gain.

Phoebe and Nick had already reached the house when she emerged from the darkness of the greenery. Briana blinked at the muted light from the veranda lamps. She took the shallow steps on the run and her sandals echoed on the planking. Phoebe already had a red and white checked tablecloth in her hands for the evening meal on the veranda.

'Let me do that, Phoebe!' Briana held out her hand.

Phoebe viewed her with amusement. 'I'm not on my last legs yet. You can get the rest of the things we need, if you like. Cutlery is in the top drawer, next to the sink, and the plates and dishes are in the glass fronted cabinet, above the fridge.'

His tall figure stood watching from the muted shadows and Briana felt that Nick Thornton was studying her; a faint flush spread over her creamy skin and she averted her glance. Her eyes concentrated on the swaying palms near the veranda and the bordering greenery. The sound of his cap landing on a vacant chair made her look again. 'I'll fix the drinks.'

Phoebe nodded. 'You know where. A whisky and soda for me . . . Briana?'

Thinking about Phoebe's meagre income, she said, 'Water, please.'

He and Phoebe moved companionably indoors and their voices were soon indistinct. Briana followed leisurely, and in the brightness of the living room she could see him better. Briana noticed that he was lean and well proportioned; his white shorts and polo shirt were expensive; his bare arms and long legs were evenly tanned.

Briana crossed the living room to fetch the plates and cutlery from the kitchen when his back was turned. Once she'd finished laying the table, and Phoebe assured her she didn't want any more help in the kitchen, Briana ran upstairs to the bedroom. After running a comb through her hair, and refreshing her lipstick, she studied her face, the gentle curve of her eyebrows and the thick dark eyelashes in the mirror. She remembered Phoebe's remarks about him and women. However attractive and interesting he appeared to be, she was forewarned.

A slender cheroot between her long bony fingers, Phoebe leaned back, tipped her head and exhaled; the smoke floated lazily upward. She gave a

9

throaty chuckle, her mouth wide with amusement as she watched Briana's face. 'I know . . . don't look like that! I know I should give it up, but it's too late to change old habits!'

Briana shrugged philosophically. 'It's your life, not mine . . . '

Phoebe McAllister's face was thin, bronzed and lined, but there was no trace of age in the lively, close-set blue eyes. 'I've tried, believe me, but . . . it's my only vice now!'

Nick's deep voice chuckled as he asked, 'What were the others, when you were up and running? Tell us; I bet it's interesting information!'

Numerous wrinkles burrowed into the older woman's parchment skin as she smiled. Her salt-and-pepper hair was pulled back into a tidy braided plait. 'All very tame in comparison with what goes on today, I assure you!'

Nick threw back his head and gave a full-throated laugh. His dark eyes glinted in the sparse light. 'If what I hear is true, you had a colourful life in your younger days. Dad said you were a knockout!'

She looked pleased. 'Oh, your father . . . he was still wet behind the ears when I was young, how does he know!' She straightened and preened a little. 'Admittedly, I wasn't bad looking and I enjoyed myself and had a lot of fun, but it was all harmless pleasure. When I met my Sam I fell hook, line and sinker. I thought life couldn't get better and we made plans; he died six months after we got engaged. I never wanted anyone else.'

Briana let the conversation between the other two go over her head most of the time. She was content to appreciate the novelty of eating her evening meal on the veranda of Phoebe's house on Turtle Island. The dish of chicken, paprika and rice was spicy and good, but she wasn't very hungry after the long-haul flight across the Atlantic, the shorter flight to Windblown Rock Island from the mainland, and then the journey by motorboat to Turtle Island.

11

All in all, it had been a long day and she was tired. She noted that Nick ate with appetite. He and Phoebe were obviously comfortable and happy in each other's company and knew each other well. Most of the time they talked about names and places that meant nothing to her. She was glad no-one expected her to show much interest.

As if he suddenly remembered she was there, he dragged her out of her reverie to ask politely. 'How long are you staying?' He noted how tiny amber lights flickered in her hazel eyes as she looked at him.

His voice flustered her for a fraction of a second. She looked questioningly in Phoebe's direction. 'A couple of weeks, perhaps longer if Phoebe can put up with me . . . '

Phoebe brushed the words aside with a gesture of her hand.

'I have to be back for the start of next term, but I've left my return flight open.'

He nodded. 'Oh, yes! You're a teacher

in junior school, aren't you? Well that gives you plenty of time. This island is the perfect place for a vacation. I've had my eye on it since doomsday, haven't I, Phoebe? I'm still waiting for her to sell it to me.'

Briana was momentarily lost for words. She turned quickly to Phoebe. 'You're thinking of selling . . . selling Turtle Island?'

Phoebe glanced at her, surprised by the reproach in the young woman's voice. 'I haven't given it serious thought yet, but I must live from something and I may be forced into it one day, especially if I face expensive care bills. I'm covered for the usual kind of hospital treatment, but as soon as you want something extra it costs money.' She shrugged. 'If Turtle has to pass into someone else's hands, then better to someone I know, than a stranger.'

Briana switched her attention back to his tanned face and dark expressionless eyes. Her suspicions were growing, and her voice was full of surprise and censure. 'It's a beautiful place of course, I can understand why anyone would want to own it, but why do you? It's too expensive to buy for just fun. Do you want to live here? Build a house . . . ?'

His eyes were slits in the half-darkness. He heard the resentment in her voice and realised she thought he was after Phoebe's possessions. 'No. I already have a bungalow; and my business interests are all on Windblown — it wouldn't be practical to live here, I could get cut off in a storm when I'm needed elsewhere.'

Phoebe's voice offered some additional information. 'Nick is joint-owner of Zenith Airlines — they flew you in to Windblown from Miami.'

That rang a bell; the picture of a garish orange Z across her flight ticket came to mind. She searched desperately in her memory for details about Nick Thornton or his family. Briana's pleasure was fading fast. So, he was just another entrepreneur out to double what he already had — someone who was trying to amass more money and possessions than he'd ever need, or could ever use!

'Really? Are you planning to tarmac Turtle Island from one end to the other, install new airport facilities and give it all the necessary infrastructure?' Her voice sounded critical and sharp.

He gave her an indulgent smile that annoyed her. She didn't realise he'd sized her up. He remembered Phoebe telling him about all the protests and campaigns she'd been involved in — ones that mostly ended in various degrees of failure, although there had also been the occasional success. Instead of making a soothing remark, he felt an urge to provoke.

'That's a brainless idea. Anyone with sense knows that Turtle Island isn't central enough, and it isn't big enough either. Do you have the slightest idea how much room you need for a runway?' He added nonchalantly. 'Although a helicopter landing pad would be a possibility, and Turtle Island could make an ideal location for an exclusive resort, with the right kind of investment of course.'

'A . . . a resort? A holiday resort?' She was lost for words, staring at him in disbelief; she turned to Phoebe again. 'You wouldn't, would you? Let him turn it into a run-of-the mill over-developed tourist centre?'

Phoebe's bright eyes twinkled and she looked at her philosophically. 'If things carry on like the present, I'll be forced into doing something, I can't live on eggs and coconuts till I die! Nick promises that I could keep my house as long as I live no matter what happens.' She noted the angry flicker in Briana's eyes and made an attempt to contain the damage. 'Hey! Calm down, and don't climb on your high horse — nothing has been decided yet.'

Briana's eyes flashed. 'From what I've seen today, this is a wonderful, beautiful and unique place. It's unex-ploited, and it would be sacrilege to change it.'

Phoebe's voice was soft and soothing. 'Beggars can't be choosers, Briana. I'm not excited about any possible changes either, but I may not be able to keep Turtle as it is. It will change hands when I die anyway. Isn't it better for me to have a say in the choice of who gets it . . . while I can?'

Briana's voice rose. 'But . . . but there must be a better alternative?' She looked at Nick still with anger in her expression, and spat out, 'Turtle Island doesn't need a hotel, a bungalow complex, a helicopter pad, or anything like that — there must be other places that are more suited to your plans.'

For some reason he didn't understand, he continued to bait her; perhaps it was because he enjoyed watching the changing emotion in her face. Well-practised in managing competitive situations, his voice sounded calm, although an attentive listener would have noticed amusement was near the surface.

'Not near here! Anyway, what makes

you so sure you're such an analytical genius? Barely arrived — you're able to solve all the problems at the drop of a hat? You're a visitor; a tourist, like any other tourist who comes to the Caribbean for a good time. Is there one rule for you, and another for everyone else? It'd be more sensible for you to think about the facts first; think about the situation from Phoebe's viewpoint and weigh up all the pros and cons, before you open your mouth.'

Clenching her teeth, she knew he was right, but she cleared her throat and flashed him a look of indignation. 'I am not just a holidaymaker looking for a good time in the Caribbean. My grandmother and Phoebe were school-friends, life-long friends . . . '

'Hold it!' He held up his hand to silence her. His voice was uncompromising. 'I know all that! I've heard all about you, your family and I even met your grandmother. What difference does it make? You are not an environmental angel with a magic wand. Turtle

Island is Turtle Island, and a tourist is a tourist. One tourist or fifty, what's the difference? Why do you want to keep Turtle exclusively for the chosen few?'

Briana was irritated, especially because he knew more about her than she about him. It was also news that her grandmother had met him. Gran had never mentioned him — or perhaps she had, and she hadn't taken enough notice?

Nick Thornton was an unusual, forceful personality, and Phoebe had known him all his life. The more Briana knew about him, the easier it would make it for her to develop the right kind of strategy. She tried to suppress the anger in her voice, and countered.

'People like me who respect the environment don't cause intentional damage. Dozens of holidaymakers who only come for a good time are the ones who don't care how much damage they do.' After a pause because her voice was getting hectic, she managed to quell her indignation a little and went on.

'I'd react the same way about plans to change this place, no matter who owns it, or who wants to buy it. What right has anyone to make a tourist bedlam out of Turtle Island or to change something so perfect? Nowadays there are too many people whose only aim is to grow rich at the cost of the environment, and it seems that you're just another!'

Bright spots burned on her cheeks. His face was hidden in the shadows thrown by the overhead lamp, and she noticed that his skin was stretched over his cheekbones. Briana interpreted it as a sign of anger. She didn't realise he was trying not to laugh at her quixotic defence of an island she hadn't seen until a few hours ago.

He liked the place as it was, and even if the selling price would soak up most of his money reserves, he knew that he'd keep it intact if he could.

'It's not mine yet, and even if it was, who knows what I'd decide in the end? Let's not quarrel over a potential castle in the air. Perhaps you can give me some sensible, constructive ideas what I should do with it?'

Phoebe sighed inwardly. She hadn't reckoned that Briana would start an environmental crusade on Turtle Island, or that she'd find anything worth championing! It was too bad of Nick to bait her. It was like watching children in kindergarten. 'Hey! Break it up you two!'

Briana looked at him but couldn't see his face. She was tired, and arguing with someone like him needed her full concentration; she pushed back her chair and got up. She'd talk things through with Phoebe in the morning.

'I suppose, we'll agree to differ and leave it there . . . for the moment. If you'll excuse me . . . I'm tired!' She gave him a quick nod, and then placed her hand on Phoebe's shoulder and bent to kiss her cheek. 'I'll take my dishes into the kitchen. Don't bother with the washing-up tonight, we'll do it tomorrow.'

Phoebe patted her hand. 'I'll put things to soak. And don't worry; I haven't decided anything yet. Nick and I have talked about the possibility for years, but I'm still playing with the idea. Sleep well, and as long as you can.'

2

The sun was sending speckled beams of bright sunshine through the closed lattice shutters when Briana woke. A quick look at her wristwatch told her it was only just gone five o'clock. The room was welcomingly cool as her bare feet walked across the polished planks to where her unpacked suitcase lay open, in front of the simple wooden wardrobe. She looked at it and shrugged; it could wait until she'd realised her desire of being alone on that beach, and swimming in the turquoise waters.

Stretching with contentment, she looked at her reflection in the mirror above the washbasin; she automatically brushed her hair, and splashed her face with water before she applied some moisturiser. Downstairs there was no sign of Phoebe.

Nick stood at the railing, a slight breeze from the sea rippling across his white cotton shirt. He breathed in the fresh tang of the morning air; it was the best time of the day — before other people's demands took over his life again. The darkness had lost its hold and red, orange and gold was splashed generously across a cloudless sky.

All of a sudden he spotted Briana swimming parallel to the shore, moving at a leisurely pace through the crystal waters. He figured she was heading for a big outgrowth of rock on the far side of the lagoon. He watched her progress absentmindedly for a while, before he reminded himself it was time to return to civilisation on Windblown and all its demands. His mouth curved into an unconscious smile as he remembered how she'd already branded him as a mercenary moneybags.

He was fairly certain the majority of women he knew didn't care where his wealth came from, as long as he was generous with it. He was also sure some women found him attractive because he was rich and successful — well, perhaps not just because of the money, but he knew it was an important factor of why some females were so anxious to catch his attention.

Even though Briana knew nothing about him, she'd already categorised and damned him — ever since Phoebe mentioned that he was a possible buyer for Turtle Island. He'd need all his persuasive skills to win her over. Was it worth proving he was not the local bad guy? He tilted his cap and looked across at her, his thoughts still wandering. He enjoyed his lifestyle; but he had worked hard to make the airline a viable enterprise, and to make him and the family independent. It also provided a lot of local people with employment.

He was irritated when he realised he was in the middle of justifying his own existence — he wasn't answerable to Briana Norton or anyone else; he was his own man. He waited until he saw her looking in his direction and lifted his hand politely. He turned away and went below to make final preparations for the journey back to Windblown.

Temperatures were climbing and it was wonderful to feel the soft water rippling softly across her body as she swam with gentle strokes across the lagoon. Reaching her goal she pulled herself up the coral's sharp surface. Easing down gradually, she finally found a comfortable position with a contented sigh, and then sat for a moment, arms clasped about her knees.

She'd seen his yacht was still anchored when she arrived; and he was standing on deck. She was glad that there was distance between them and no necessity for small talk; she didn't want him to spoil her first morning on Turtle Island.

After a couple of minutes of pure bliss, she sighed again. She was so lucky to be here. She slid back carefully into the water avoiding the coral's sharp surface and headed for the beach. When she had firm sand under her feet again, she resisted taking a backward look to see where his yacht was now. She made for the house with a jaunty spring in her step and was still vigorously rubbing her hair when she reached it. Phoebe was sitting in the living room enveloped in a faded cotton wrap-around and with a mug in her hand.

'Oh! Been for a swim already? Slept well?'

'Like a log!'

'Good! We can breakfast together. What do you want?'

'No fuss! I never eat much in the mornings, usually haven't enough time!'

'Right! I don't bother much either. Coffee is ready!' She raised her mug. 'There's cornflakes or toast. Help yourself!'

A few minutes later Briana finished her bowl of cereal, leaned back in the wickerwork chair stretching her arms up, and then moved forward slightly again to take her mug of coffee. She sighed. 'Oh, this is wonderful! It's just as I imagined. Gran said it was paradise, and she was right.' She clasped the mug between her hands and took a sip.

Phoebe smiled. 'Yes, she liked it here, didn't she? She spent most of the day on the veranda reading and went exploring when the temperatures dropped. She only came once, but she liked the lifestyle and loved the island. She said she'd come again as soon as she could afford it.'

A worried expression took over Briana's face. 'She was generous to a fault with other people, but not with herself. I didn't even realise that she'd borrowed money.'

Phoebe nodded understandingly. 'I did. She wrote and told me; she wanted to give you a little extra on top of your grant when you were at university. She was so sure she could pay back the loan quickly once you were established.'

'I wish I'd known, I'd have tried to stop her, or at least taken over the repayment once I started working. I wish she hadn't borrowed for my sake;

it makes me feel guilty.'

'No need for that; it was her greatest joy to know she was helping you. She didn't reckon with a stroke, she was always so healthy. What happens about paying the debt off?'

'If I can't persuade them to transfer the debt to me, the bank will probably foreclose on the house to get their money.'

'You have to find a way to keep it! Elsie wanted you to have it for security.'

'If I can, I will. The bank still hasn't decided if I'm a safe bet or not. That's why I thought that I'd better book my air-ticket now, before my account ran dry.'

Phoebe searched her pocket for cheroots and took one out, waving it questionably at Briana.

'Of course, Phoebe. Don't ask — this is your house, not mine!'

Phoebe lit the thin cigar and blew a ring of smoke contentedly. 'It's a good thing you've come. Apart from giving you time to get over Elsie's death, it's a chance for us to meet properly. When I visited her last time, you were still an au-pair in France.'

Briana leaned back into her chair and wrinkled her nose. 'Yes! By the time I finished, you were already on your way home again, and the first time you came I was too young to take much notice of Gran's friend!'

'Well you're here now, that's the main thing!'

Briana's features were animated. 'I'm really looking forward to this holi- day . . . '

'When does school start again? Stay as long as you possibly can.'

'That's generous and very kind; I hope I don't get on your nerves . . . '

Phoebe brushed some imaginary dust from the table. Her voice was brisk. 'You're very, very welcome. You paid your own fare, so you aren't beholden in any way, and you won't be a burden either. If I don't feel like your company, I'll tell you so, and leave you to your own devices. I think we'll get along fine.

You remind me of Elsie, and neither of us liked beating around the bush.'

Briana nodded. 'That's a compliment.'

Phoebe stubbed out the cheroot in the ashtray. 'I'd like to introduce you to the others, if you're ready.'

'Of course! Who exactly are the others?'

Phoebe got up. Briana put their crockery on a tray. 'There's John and his family, Terry, Madeline and their two children, and Robert and Joyce — they have two grown up sons who work, and live, on Windblown Rock. Together we make up the population of Turtle Island.' She preceded Briana into the simple, but spotlessly clean kitchen.

They stood side by side and Phoebe began to do the washing up.

Briana picked up the teacloth and waited for the first item. She hesitated, a little reluctant to mention his name. 'Nick was still there when I went for a swim.'

'Was he?'

'Well, his yacht was just about to leave I think.'

'He doesn't usually stay overnight; he's too busy to linger.'

'He runs Zenith Airlines?'

'In partnership with his father! Mind you, it wasn't a completely voluntary move. The airline was the pipe-dream of his father and his twin brother, Darren. Unfortunately Darren was killed a couple of years after the company was founded.' A cooking pot rattled as she scrubbed it vigorously. 'At that time Nick was on the brink of founding a ship chartering business but he dumped his plans to help save the airline. His parents, sister-in-law and two nephews were dependant on it for an income.'

'How long ago was that?' Phoebe's disclosure softened the picture she'd fabricated of Nick Thornton, but it didn't erase the image of the iron-fisted capitalist.

'Oh, let's see. He's roughly thirty-four now, so it must be seven or eight years ago. The business tottered for a while, but apparently it's doing well now.'

'Is he married?'

Phoebe chuckled. 'No. Though it's not for the want of trying! He has his following, or so I gather.'

She wondered why she cared. The draining board was empty. Briana shook out the cloth vigorously, and hung it up. 'So, that's it. I'm ready to meet the others if you like.'

Phoebe dried her hands. 'Yes. It won't take long. Take a hat; the sun gets hot from now on and you're not used to it'

'Haven't got one.'

'Try the upstairs hall cupboard.'

Briana found a battered boater. It had seen better days, but she put it jauntily on the back of her head and smiled at her reflection in the mirror. Phoebe was waiting; they set off along one of the paths behind the house.

The other island inhabitants were friendly, welcoming and uncompli-cated; they were also curious about

Phoebe's visitor. John wasn't there, he took his own and Terry and Madeline's children, to Windblown every day so that they could attend school. He worked in the small harbour every day for a small, but life-saving wage and brought the children back late in the afternoon.

Robert and Joyce's sons worked, and lived, on Windblown and they each supplied their parents with a little money so that they could continue to exist comfortably on Turtle.

All their incomes were fairly unpredictable, and it wasn't easy to understand why they were so cheerful and optimistic, but Briana could appreciate that contentment couldn't be measured in income. This was a different kind of environment, they were happy despite the problems; and they also cared about each other.

Phoebe and Briana accepted some cool fresh coconut juice, and the women asked her questions about her job, her home, and her family. When their questions ran out, the conversation became general. After a while Briana got up to take a stroll around.

The huts were in a wide circle. The planked walls had a weathered appearance, but they were in a healthy condition. The roofs were of corrugated iron, although Briana was delighted to see one covered in traditional palm-leaf.

The whole area was tidy and well kept; someone had recently swept the ground, faint lines were still visible on the brown surface where they'd been busy with a brush.

Nearby, through the gaps in the greenery, there was a pathway to a small sun-beaten beach; the trail to the crest of the beach had been hardened by the constant pounding of numerous feet.

An indefinable sweet tropical smell mingled with the salty tang from the sea as Briana emerged on to the seashore. An unpretentious boat with the name, *Sally Ann*, painted askew in bright blue on its bow was leaning sideways on the coral sands.

Briana was awed; the island was breathtaking. She thought about the possibility that Nick Thornton or someone else might change all this, and make bungalow facilities or put up a feudal hotel. It was beyond comprehension!

It was hot by the time they got back to the house, so she made herself comfortable on the shady veranda with a paperback. Phoebe went for her afternoon siesta. Briana read for a while, quenching her thirst with iced water. Eventually she put on her hat and set off along one of the paths behind the house. She chose one at random — from the look of it, it was one that wasn't in regular use.

After a few minutes she came across four dilapidated huts. They were huddled together beneath sheltering palm trees and surrounded by tropical vegetation. She climbed the steps of the nearest one, pushed open the door and stepped carefully inside. There were two large, and one small room.

In the smaller room there was a simple pot stove with a rusty door and in the corner was a dilapidated sink. In another, sunlight fought its way through gaps in the roof, a broken chair lay on its side, and there were some pieces of wood covered in fine red dust.

The third room contained two bottles, neglected and forgotten, lying on their sides against the wall. Most of the window-panes were intact, but the veranda's railing was loose, and the planking was flawed.

She looked back at the huts absent-mindedly for a while, before continuing along the pathway, lined with bright red hibiscus bushes.

She wasn't surprised to hear the sound of the ocean ahead of her, but Briana was caught off guard to find herself suddenly on the edge of a mangrove. She'd only ever seen mangrove trees in pictures before; their shapes were bizarre and fascinating.

Some of the trees had thick trunks, while others were spindly and weak looking specimens; they all had angled branches and a maze of aerial roots. She knew mangroves grew where the tides move in and out, and that they were regularly covered by salt water.

She left her sandals on dry ground and walked between the roots. With every step she took, she sank deeper into the muddy sediment. Her feet came free with a soft sucking sound and her lower legs were soon covered in mud. At last she reached the edge of a group of trees, and was grateful for the cool breezes blowing from the ocean. She pulled herself up on to one of the thicker trunks and straddled the bough, swinging her dirty legs as she looked out to sea. It was wonderful here, and quite unique.

Phoebe was relaxing when she got back.

Briana sat down and tilted her head back. 'How long have the huts been empty, Phoebe?' Briana explained where she'd been.

'Oh, those! I'm not sure six, seven . . . perhaps eight years.'

'What happened? Why are they empty?'

'People moved to Windblown. John lived there once, but he moved when he was the only one left. It wasn't much fun for his wife to walk half the length of the island to talk to others, or for his children to play with the other kids, so . . . '

'They're yours? The huts?'

'Yes, everything is mine; Turtle Island belongs to me.'

'It's been in your family for generations hasn't it? Gran told me there was rumour about pirates and hidden treasure.'

Phoebe gave a boisterous laugh. 'Rubbish! Every Caribbean island has those kinds of rumours. Pirates probably visited us, but as far as we know they left nothing. Sorry to disappoint you, love!'

Briana quelled a tiny twinge of

disenchantment. 'And how did your family come to own the island?'

'Family tradition says our forefather was a sailor, perhaps even a pirate; one who fell in love with a local girl and became a landlubber. He paid a pittance to the Spanish crown for the island, and it's been in the family ever since. I don't have any heirs, so it all ends with me.'

Briana looked contemplatively towards the greenery bordering the veranda. 'Don't you mind the idea of someone turning the island into a fairground?'

'Fairground? Oh you mean the possibility that Nick might buy Turtle?' She grinned. 'I wondered when you'd bring that up again. I can't imagine it overrun by strangers, and I don't honestly think Nick would go haywire. I've been lucky up to now — John and the others keep things under control, but some problems can't be ignored forever.'

'Don't sell, Phoebe!'

3

Phoebe sighed and her eyes clouded over. 'That's easier said than done. I'm facing old age with practically no income. I wouldn't say this to many people, but I'll be honest with you. I'm not afraid of dying; just afraid that I won't be able to keep my dignity when I'm old.' An anxious expression governed her features.

Briana dropped her lashes to hide her concern. When she lifted her eyes again, they were full of sympathy. She touched Phoebe's arm lightly and said, 'Don't worry. We'll think of something. There's a way out of this, I'm sure.' Her thoughts wandered back to the deserted huts. 'Do you think I could go over to Windblown with John tomorrow — just to have a look around, and get some postcards?'

Phoebe straightened, probably glad

41

to change the subject. 'Of course! Just be at the jetty by eight-thirty tomorrow morning. Enough about me, and Turtle Island! Tell me something about what you've been doing recently. Tell me about your latest passionate affair, about Prince Charming, about your dilly-dallying.'

Briana tossed her hair across her shoulders in a gesture of dismissal. 'Passionate affair? Lord, I wish I could! Prince Charming died out with the dinosaurs, and I need a dictionary to study the exact meaning of dilly-dallying before commenting on that.'

Phoebe's voice cackled. 'What . . . no-one promising; not even a silhouette on the horizon? You're attractive, intelligent, and you have a steady, respectable job. I don't get it. Why ever not?'

Briana wrinkled her nose. 'In your heyday women were merely content to be a man's docile companion. Expectations and moral standards were different too, and men more or less had the final say in everything. Modern women want careers, and don't want to be tied down before they choose to do so themselves. But that means they are harder to please when it comes to finding the right partner — they need someone with modern attitudes and who is prepared to compromise.'

Phoebe's voice didn't give anything away, although she wasn't sure if Briana would answer. 'But you fell for Jason, didn't you? According to Elsie he was a very nice and charming lad.'

Briana's face was impassive. 'Jason? Yes, I thought I loved him. And yes, he was charming, good-looking and nice! Trouble was that Myra thought so too.'

Phoebe's voice tried to reassure. 'You're not pigeonholing all other men because of how he behaved, are you?'

'Oh, of course not, but it hurt at the time — she was my friend, and Jason and I were almost engaged.' She made a point of dismissal with a shrug of her shoulders. 'He couldn't have really loved me or he wouldn't have dropped me so easily for someone else. Looking back, I'm glad now. I suspect it mightn't have worked anyway; in some respect we were like chalk and cheese.'

'I hope it doesn't leave you resentful? I sometimes wonder if growing up with your gran was the right solution for you.'

Briana tilted her head and smiled. 'What do you mean? Gran was wonderful.'

Phoebe brushed aside the comment impatiently with her hand. 'Of course she was! I'm talking about her attitude to your dad. Perhaps she gave you the wrong set of values; and instilled too many misgivings about men.'

'Oh, Phoebe! I was happier with Gran than I'd have been with Dad — especially after he married Marcia. I'm not a man-hater because of my father. I don't blame him. At the time he couldn't cope with Mum's death and me. Gran supplied all the love I needed. If men are likeable I like them, if not I don't. I'm not more mixed up than average.'

Phoebe gave her a quick understanding smile. She paused a moment, and stared out across the veranda, to where the sea shimmered in the distance through the palms. 'Put it down to experience, Briana. Life isn't always kind, but mistakes like Jason make it easier to recognise real love when it happens.'

'You're too romantic, that's your trouble. I'm a 27-year-old single female. I enjoy teaching, and don't worry about meeting the right man. If it happens, fine — if not, life has other compensations.'

Phoebe grunted a disbelieving, *has it*? 'Elsie mentioned another man's name in her last letter, just before she died.'

Hearing her grandmother's name, Briana's eyes clouded. 'That was Francis, I expect.'

Phoebe's eyes lit up as hope burgeoned. 'Tell me more!'

45

'There's not much to tell . . . An uncomplicated, undemanding man.'

'And . . . ?'

'Nice . . . but too predictable . . . he's exasperating! A gardener, with his own gardening centre.'

'A gardener? Good heavens! Dungarees and Wellingtons?'

Briana's hazel eyes sparkled. 'Jeans and solid shoes! But he's nice, and we both care about the countryside and the environment — excluding that there wasn't much else that united us though. To be fair, his business doesn't leave him much time for anything else. Francis needs a girlfriend who is just as enthusiastic about re-potting plants and designing gardens as he is himself.'

'So he's not special?'

Briana shook her head decisively. 'Sorry to spoil your romantic illusions!'

Next morning she sat with John and his two little girls in his small motorboat on the early morning crossing to Windblown. She had enough professional curiosity to flip through the

46

children's textbooks. The two girls were eight and ten, the age group she taught back home. They were lively intelligent children, and seemed to enjoy school, so their teacher was doing a good job.

Pushing her hair back from her face, she asked John, 'What happens when the sea is too rough?'

John smiled; his strong white teeth were in stark contrast to the beautiful chocolate colour of his skin. 'If it's turbulent before we leave, we stay at home. If it turns stormy when the children are in school and the return journey is too risky, we have relatives in the town and they stay overnight with them.'

Briana had to speak loudly over the sound of the engine, but the crossing was short; they'd taken less than ten minutes. John was already throttling the engine, and they were approaching the entrance to the small harbour. 'Do you get storms often?'

'Depends on the season, and some years are worse than others. The occasional storm isn't so bad, but hurricanes can be life-threatening. They're really frightening and unpredictable, and cause a lot of damage. You can only close the shutters and pray that it won't be a direct hit. We've been lucky on Turtle for a couple of years now.' He threw a rope up on to the wooden jetty and jumped up with agility; he quickly knotted it to one of the rings sunk into the wooden planks. The two girls sprang with accustomed skill from the boat, but Briana was grateful for the help from his steadying hand.

'What time do you go back?'

'Round about four-thirty! I work in the warehouse, and I finish in time to take the kids home when school finishes. The town isn't big, so you can't get lost.'

'Any recommendation on where I can eat?'

'I'd say Miss Betty's on Main Street, next to the Post Office. It's quite safe around here.'

At first glance, the town didn't have anything special to recommend it, but soon the colours, the exotic smells, and the unique appearance of buildings that lined the streets caught Briana's imagination. The majority of buildings were small and squat, with simple windows and walls that flaunted a multitude of bright colours; nearly all of them had corrugated roofs painted in red or orange.

After strolling along the sun-drenched sidewalks for a while, just looking and watching, Briana found herself near the Post Office — a Victorian style building. It was painted pink with the embellishments picked out in white. She remembered John's recommendation — Miss Betty's.

Outwardly Miss Betty's looked like any other coffee bar; it had small bistro tables with artificial marble tops and black cane chairs. Briana sat down at one of the tables in the corner. Only a few tables were occupied, and a waitress sauntered across to her.

'Hi, honey! What can I get you?' Her brown cheeks shone like shiny apples and her perfect white teeth formed themselves into a wonderful smile.

Briana smiled back. 'A cappuccino and a cheese sandwich please?'

'Sure thing! Coming straight up!' She wiped the surface of the table with a cloth, even though everything was spotlessly clean. 'Tourist?'

'Yes. I'm staying on Turtle Island.'

The smile blossomed once again. 'With Phoebe? You're her visitor from the UK? Phoebe comes in here often. She mentioned you last time she was in. Like it?'

Briana laughed softly. 'I only arrived two days ago, but I love it so far.'

'Good! Give her my love — from Maud! She's one of my favourite people. No messing about with Phoebe! I like that . . . I'll get your order.'

The coffee machine hissed and protested, but Maud had it under control and she was soon back with a large white cup topped with creamy froth and a sandwich so large that it was in danger of falling off the edge of the plate.

Briana decided Maud was the perfect person to ask — probably a mine of information. 'Is there an internet shop locally?'

'Hmm! I don't know. The hotel isn't the right place — they are a funny bunch over there, and only cater for their own guests. The Post Office definitely doesn't have that kind of facility.' She laughed. 'They still count in coconuts!' Still smiling, she turned to her friend behind the counter, and yelled, 'Hey Gloria! She wants an internet shop — know some place?'

Gloria stopped cutting some fresh sandwiches and considered the problem. She shook her head. 'No idea!'

One of the other customers with a Rasta hairstyle shouted, 'There's one on Hobart Street!'

Briana looked across at the man gratefully. 'Perfect! Where is Hobart Street?'

Maud took charge again. 'It's ten minutes from here. Starting outside the main entrance to the Post Office you go straight down the Main Street to the right until the second set of traffic lights, then turn left — no I tell a lie — turn right and you're in Hobart Street, there's a gas station on the corner.'

Walking back from the internet-café she felt pleased. Her friend had been online, and answered straight away; she'd promised to make enquiries and gather information. Briana hoped that she might be able to tell Phoebe about her idea in a day or two. She still had a few hours to spare before she had to meet John again, so she bought some postcards and stamps.

She sauntered past what seemed at first to be a tourist office, but glancing up she found *Zenith Airlines* written in bold orange letters across the windows. She increased her speed to pass quickly, but the entrance door opened just as she was about to go by. Her breath caught in her throat when she almost collided with Nick as he hurried down the steps. She automatically swerved to one side as she registered him coming.

He muttered hastily. 'Sorry!' Then eyebrows fractionally raised, he met her glance as his interest sharpened on recognition. He was first to speak; she didn't realise he was trying to stop himself grinning at the picture of her in Phoebe's dilapidated straw hat. 'Briana! What are you doing here?'

The sight of him made her freeze for a second, and she coloured slightly. She was flustered and she felt annoyed with herself at the effect he had on her. She fished around for a plausible answer to his question. 'Oh! . . . You know, the usual thing! I . . . I promised to send friends postcards as soon as I arrived — there aren't any postcards on Turtle!'

He looked amused. 'No that's true — there aren't are there?'

Lost for conversation, she gestured towards the building. 'Your business?' She was flummoxed and thought back to how they'd been at daggers drawn a day or two ago.

'Part of it! It's not mine; it's ours! Zenith Airlines started from here, and for some reason I'm still reluctant to close it down and integrate it into the headquarters on the main highway close to the airport. They organise the freight business between the islands here.'

She nodded absentmindedly. 'Oh, I see.' She hoped he'd say goodbye and leave. He didn't. The trouble was she was torn in two directions because he excited her more than she cared to admit. 'Well, nice to see you! I'm sure you're very busy, so I won't keep you.'

Nonchalantly he dawdled. 'Not particularly! What are you planning to do?' Her hair was glowing in the sunshine, and he was fascinated by the gold-flecks in her eyes.

'I'll stroll back in the direction of the harbour, and wander around for a bit.'

'Going back with John?'

'Yes.'

'Bought your postcards?'

'Yes.'

He looked at his wristwatch. 'Right. That leaves you three hours to kill. Like to see Zenith Airlines from the inside?' His eyes twinkled as he waited for her to answer.

4

'I . . . Well . . . I was about to . . . ' He tucked his hand under her elbow and propelled her towards a red convertible parked nearby in the shade of some straggly palms. He threw the passenger door open and she got in.

Throwing a briefcase on to the narrow back seat, he slid into the driver's seat and indicated she should fix her safety belt. Briana had already decided that the motorised population of Windblown followed unique traffic regulations because driver skills were erratic to say the least.

The car radio supplied soft music and the warm air played with her hair. She sank back into the comfortable upholstery and ignored the warnings from her brain about *consorting with the enemy*. Nick was out to flaunt his position and demonstrate his affluence

— well, let him!

Two hours later some of her resolution had crumbled. She'd admired the steel and glass administration building, wandered through the hangars, met his father, been introduced to Sally, his sister-in-law, met some mechanics, pilots, office staff, and even seen how a troupe of cleaners got a plane ready for its next flight. She walked with him back to his office; a large room with floor-length windows overlooking the courtyard and main entrance below.

The exclusive office furnishing was opulent by anyone's standards. Although Briana tried to remain indifferent, she admitted to herself that the small airline was clearly a vibrant and going concern.

It wouldn't stop her trying to prevent him getting Turtle Island; if anything, all she'd seen increased her determination not to give way. He motioned towards a leather chair facing the desk. She crossed her legs at the ankles, leaned back, and met his eyes across the polished surface. 'I'm impressed . . . with Zenith.' She reached forward and picked up a glass he'd just filled with some cold orange juice.

'Really? From the expression on your face, I get the impression you're trying not to show any kind of approval!' One corner of his mouth curled. 'Too many signs of affluence is probably like having to swallow poison for someone like you!'

'Someone like me?' Briana raised her eyebrows fractionally. She looked around and gestured with a hand. 'Oh, I suppose you mean if I think all of this is necessary? You're right of course! The aeroplane hangars, the workshop, the canteen, and the office — I can understand why you need those, but this?' She made another vague gesture to include the whole room. 'Wouldn't it be fairer to use what this cost to give your employees a bonus instead?'

His dark brown eyes stared at her unblinking. 'Perhaps . . . but my family are not running a social club, and we pay our employees a lot more than the majority of companies do around here. If we didn't have suitable representative offices, we wouldn't pick up so many contracts.'

Briana realised he was right. Zenith Airlines and Nick Thornton were doing well because they were successful at impressing people. She forced lightness into her voice. 'Yes, I suppose so! This is a foreign world to me; a teacher doesn't normally have much to do with cut-throat competition.'

A quick knock caught their attention, and the door opened. Ron Thornton headed straight towards Briana, waving papers around.

'Well, young lady, what do you think of the place?'

Briana liked the older man instinctively; she'd found it very easy to chat to him when he showed her around the mechanical workshop, his enthusiasm for his work shone through.

'I was just telling Nick that it's all very impressive.'

Ron nodded, and handed his son the sheets of papers, adding, 'We've finished number five, so it can go back into service tomorrow.'

'Good!' Nick was taller and leaner than his father, and whereas Ron Thornton clearly felt at home in dungarees, his son couldn't be mistaken for anything but a polished executive. Nick looked down briefly at the documents and said, 'I'll sort these out and get things organised after I've taken Briana back to the harbour.'

Ron Thornton gave her a friendly smile. 'Hey, Briana, my wife and I are having a barbecue on Saturday. Just a few friends, how about you and Phoebe?'

She was agreeably surprised and smiled back. 'I'll ask Phoebe. She can phone you.'

'No! That's too much bother when people live on different islands like we do around here! The rule is to invite everyone, and have enough extra provisions. We'd like to see you;

wouldn't we Nick? It'll give you a chance to meet some other people.'

Nick's expression was detached, but he nodded. Briana mused he could hardly do otherwise. 'Right.' She stood up. 'Will you call me a taxi, please, Nick?'

His answer was curt and defied any argument. 'I brought you here; I'll take you back.' He headed towards the door without a backward glance.

His father went with them chatting to Briana on the way. They parted at the main entrance door. 'Thanks for the invitation, Mr Thornton.'

'The name's Ron — and don't thank me, I only showed you the workshop, Nick did the rest.'

She smiled, and hurried to catch up with Nick.

Once she was settled in his car, she relaxed at the prospect she'd soon be free of Nick Thornton's company. She was still very sceptical about his motives for visiting Phoebe and she felt on edge, but for some unexplainable reason she couldn't help liking him — just a little. He was an interesting and intelligent man; and he was congenial, helpful, and very relaxed.

The engine purred, and the warm air ruffled her hair again. It was easier to ask him questions when he was concentrating on the road ahead. 'You know an awful lot about me, and I'm at a distinct disadvantage. Tell me something about yourself.'

He smiled lazily. 'Phoebe mentioned you all the time. I have a good memory for what people tell me. What do you want to know? What age I was potty-trained? The name of my first girlfriend?'

She ignored his bantering. 'Phoebe told me you intended to run a ship charter company at one time, but you dropped the idea when your brother died. You clearly still love sailing, so have you given up that idea completely?'

His hands shifted uneasily on the steering wheel, and he continued to stare ahead. 'Some days . . . the hectic days . . . then I think about what it would have been like, but it's just a passing fancy these days. My family needed my support at that time, and it wasn't a sacrifice. Zenith functions well now, and Sally and the two boys have a secure future. I owed that to my brother, he'd have done the same for me.'

'What was he like? He was your twin wasn't he?'

'Darren? Yes, we weren't identical twins, but it was like losing part of myself when he was killed. I still can't believe I'll never see him again. He was a passionate pilot, a great father and a nice guy. Sally coped very well, and the kids are a credit to her. She's going out with one of the pilots at present, and I wish her luck. Brett is a nice guy, and the kids seem to like him a lot. That's great; it helps Sally accept the new situation.'

★ ★ ★

Later, Phoebe looked sceptical but tried to sound interested. 'You really think a scheme like this can work?'

Briana nodded, her eyes sparkling. 'A friend of mine works in tourism, and Jean knows a lot of people in the business. I explained about the situation here, and asked her to explore if the idea was possible or not. She talked it through with professionals who know about the pitfalls and they said it had a very good chance of success — although they'd need more details, more photos, etc. to check it out thoroughly. If you really decided to give it a try, Jean will get them to work out a fair financial deal.'

'An income from four or five huts? Would it be worth the bother? It certainly won't make me rich.'

'Do you want to be rich? You just need a little more income, a steady income, don't you? It'd at least generate enough money to keep your head well above water, and provide some of the others on the island with a small income as well.' Phoebe stirred uneasily in her chair, but looked more interested, so Briana ploughed on. 'Nowadays people will pay good money to get away from the maddening crowd. You'd be surprised how many people are looking for somewhere like Turtle, just to have a couple of weeks of comparative peace and quiet.'

'The huts are falling apart! Where's the money coming from to put them right? No-one has lived in them for years; they're pretty dilapidated.'

'People won't expect luxury when they book an environmental holiday, that's the great thing about this scheme. The huts aren't in such a bad state of repair; they need some patching, cleaning and painting. I'll contribute as much help towards that as I can manage. I'm sure Terry will help, especially with any heavy jobs; you can always give him a couple of extra dollars when the scheme takes off.'

'The offer in the brochures have to

make it clear that it isn't the place to come to expect four showers a day, or a luxury holiday. If necessary you'll have to ration the water supply — but I'm positive that anyone who wants this kind of holiday is someone who only wants basic comforts.' She paused. 'That's a thought — have you got enough water?'

Phoebe answered quickly; her interest was growing now. She nodded. 'We've several underground cisterns; they're fed with rainwater from this roof, and from a long wide ditch my father dynamited out of the coral on the north side of the island — its lowest point.' Phoebe was looking more optimistic.

She paused thoughtfully. 'I must say your idea is tempting. It'd be ideal if there were only a couple of visitors at a time. I'd get some extra income without too much disruption, and the others will get something from the scheme too.'

'Don't expect too much money. I'll get some definite figures from my friends, and then you'll have a better idea. It must be an improvement on what you have now.' Briana paused and then rushed on again. 'Of course you still have the alternative of selling the island to Nick, or someone else. If you did that, your financial worries would be over, but you couldn't stop any future plans they might have.'

Phoebe sat, her thin fingers tensed in her lap, and a more worried expression in her eyes. 'Yes, I realise that. You know that I like Nick very, very much, he's like a son and he's the kind of man you can't help liking, but I've always been in control on Turtle. I don't know how I'd cope with someone else, even Nick, making all the decision over my head.'

Pushing her hair back from her temples, Briana tried to sound unbiased and sensible. 'Think it over, Phoebe; and take your time. Think about the pros and cons. You may be forced into making decisions sometime in the future, so perhaps this is the chance to do something now. You can always fall back on Nick's offer if it doesn't work.'

Phoebe bit her lip. 'This scheme of yours . . . I won't have to get too involved, will I? I'm not getting any younger. I can handle things now perhaps, but next year . . . the year after — who knows?'

Briana nodded. 'Once we've got through the routine of the first visitors, I'm sure it would follow the same kind of pattern thereafter. You only need to be the figurehead, be the owner, and keep an eye on things. Let Terry, or Joyce, or Madeleine handle the actual fetching, and installing of visitors etc, and give them a small wage for doing so. Once a routine is established you probably only need do as much, or as little, as you want . . . and you'll be able to decide about Turtle Island until the day you die.'

Phoebe studied the younger woman's face pensively and her expression brightened at the prospect. 'That would be wonderful and I'm sure Joyce,

Madeleine and the others would welcome the chance to earn a little money. The only place for them to find work is on Windblown, and there are too many unemployed already fighting for those jobs.'

Briana nodded. 'You could offer a self-catering holiday with just the cleaning, or one with breakfast, or with breakfast and lunch, or perhaps even one with everything included — adjusting the price accordingly of course.'

Phoebe's eyes widened. 'Breakfast? Lunch? Dinner? Briana, I can't cook for other people any more. I don't like cooking much, never have!'

Briana laughed. 'I know that. I bet Madeleine and John's wife would be prepared to do it for a wage though, wouldn't they? We could use one of the huts as a central unit. The women could use the bigger room as a dining room and we could make a kitchen in the other. They could cater according to visitors' demands.'

Briana didn't mention it again for a

couple of days, giving Phoebe time to think about it in peace. She went over to Windblown to get in touch with her friend, Jean, and asked her to put some definite facts and figures together. She spent the rest of the week lazing on the beach, making lethargic notes about what she thought the scheme needed to make it feasible.

She read her way through a couple of paperbacks, swam in the waters of the empty green lagoon and mused about what it would be like to live and work here for ever. She began to look forward to the weekend and the coming barbeque at Nick's parents home.

5

Phoebe had paused for a moment when Briana passed on Ron Thornton's invitation, but then she said, 'Why not?' To be honest, Phoebe seldom felt the need to wander far from Turtle these days unless there was a pushing reason, but she was glad to give Briana the chance to meet some other people. It must be boring for her to spend all her time on Turtle Island with an old woman.

Briana wondered if Nick would be there; the invitation was from his parents, and perhaps there'd only be his parents' friends and acquaintances. At first Phoebe had tentatively suggested they could stay with Mary overnight in town, but when Briana asked why they couldn't ask John to pick them up at midnight, Phoebe was relieved — the older she got, the more she appreciated her own bed. John said it was no problem and he'd be there.

They took a taxi from the harbour; it cleared the noisy built-up area of the town quickly and made easy progress. They turned off down a rough track until they came to a halt in front of a low-pitched bungalow that was built to stand the storms that swept the island.

A figure came bustling round the angle of the building, and his face split into a smile as Phoebe slowly emerged from the vehicle.

'Phoebe! I didn't really think you'd come. Good on ye girl! It's been too long; great to see you made the effort!'

Phoebe nodded and grinned, and stated with complete honesty. 'I wanted Briana to meet some other people, otherwise I wouldn't have bothered.'

Ron Thornton chuckled and turned to Briana who was paying the taxidriver. 'I'm so very glad you came to Turtle Island, Briana. Come and meet my wife, and the others.'

He waited patiently, adjusting his

sprightly step to stay at Phoebe's side as they wandered towards the sound of music and voices on the other side of the building facing the sea.

Briana shook hands with a lot of people, and initially tried to remember names, but soon gave up — there were too many. When they reached a set of French windows, a woman with a modern short hair cut came out carrying a tray with empty glasses. Ron Thornton threw his arm in a casual gesture of affection around his wife's shoulder.

'Ah, there you are, love! Look who's here . . . Phoebe! And this young lady is Briana. I mentioned that Nick showed her around Zenith the other day, didn't I?'

Nick's mother looked at Briana with dark blue eyes that were bright, interested and curious. 'Hello! Yes, I remember Ron mentioning you! You're very welcome, Briana, what a nice name . . . and Phoebe, how nice! Lovely to see you again, we don't see enough of you any more. How are you?'

'Hmm! I'm getting older fast, my dear, the effort to go anywhere is just too much. On Turtle I feel like a juicy mussel clinging to its rock; take me off, and I just shrivel up.'

Charlotte Thornton put the tray down on a nearby table and said firmly, 'It's not good for you to be on your own so much, Phoebe; we all need company now and then. Mary's waiting for you; she wants to tell you the latest gossip. She's over there, by the flower beds.' Charlotte nodded vaguely in the direction of a group of people on the edge of the gathering. Phoebe nodded, and glanced at Briana.

Nick's mother solved Phoebe's unspoken dilemma. 'I'll take care of Briana!'

Nick's mother turned to Briana and took a closer look. 'I'll take you across to the younger people!' She tucked her hand under Briana's elbow and guided her gently down some wide wooden steps, through hibiscus and poinsettia bushes, and across the soft warm sand to the firmer area of the beach bordering the ocean.

As they progressed Charlotte Thornton chatted pleasantly with her guest. 'How do you like the islands? Enjoying your visit?'

Briana nodded enthusiastically and smiled. 'Very much! Who wouldn't! It's absolutely wonderful. This is all like a page out of a fantastic travel brochure.'

Charlotte Thornton gave her a pleased look. 'It does have negative sides, like the storms and high unemployment, but on the whole, I agree. I've always loved living here. The only thing that's ever made me miserable was Darren's death. I still haven't got over that. I never will, I suppose.'

'Yes. Nick told me. That must have been horrific for you all, especially for Sally.'

She nodded. 'She's been wonderful through it all. I'm sure the children helped her to keep going, but she was absolutely shattered for months and months. She functioned because they needed her. Thank heavens for the boys; they're a real credit to her.' She sighed and straightened her shoulders. 'Darren would have been so proud of them. You know Sally?'

'Yes . . . I met her briefly, in the company the other day.'

She nodded. 'Oh yes, the day Nick showed you around. Nick met you at Phoebe's first, didn't he? He's been visiting Phoebe for donkey's years. They get on like a house on fire.'

Briana nodded mutely.

'The younger people always end up on the beach; avoiding the older generation I expect. I'm sure Sally will take you under her wing.'

They were approaching people standing on the sand or sitting on the nearby rocks; nearby was a small table loaded with various bottles and glasses. A tall figure detached itself from the group and strolled in their direction.

'Ah! Here comes Nick!'

Her pulse jumped around erratically and she tried not to appear befuddled as he drew closer. She exchanged smiles and touched his hand briefly in greeting.

'Hi! Come and join us! Everything OK up at the house, Mom?'

His mother gave him an affectionate glance. 'Fine! I don't know if your father wants help with the barbecue, but knowing how he likes to pretend that he's the world's top expert on burgers and steaks, it's not very likely.'

Nick gave a bluff laugh and his mouth took on an infectious grin.

Charlotte Thornton chuckled. 'I'll leave Briana with you and get back to the older generation.' She noticed a fleeting change in Nick's expression as his eyes focussed on Briana.

Charlotte turned towards the bungalow again and thought about Ron's references to Li Sun, an American-Chinese who worked for the company's American advertising agency. Li came to Windblown from time to time, to coordinate strategies, but lately she seemed to be around more often than necessary, and Nick and she had been seen about town several times recently.

Charlotte had met her, and she was here this evening. Li was beautiful to look at, polite, and pleasing, but Charlotte had niggling doubts about whether Li really liked Nick for what he was, or if she saw him as her ticket to a comfortable lifestyle.

Briana studied Nick's face and forced herself to remain calm. 'How are you?' It was a superfluous remark, but all that jumped to mind.

His dark brown eyes seemed almost black as they regarded her, and she saw a secretive smile soften his lips. 'Fine! And you?'

She nodded silently.

'Good.' He held out his hand, palm up, and she hesitatingly placed hers in his.

'Come and meet the others!'

He introduced her to several people and she was genuinely pleased to find herself standing next to Sally again, and to receive a warm, welcoming smile from her. He released her hand again.

'Nice to see you, Briana! Enjoying your vacation, I hope?' Sally nodded to a tall man at her side with the information. 'This is Brett.'

A pleasant looking man with a slow warm smile, acknowledged Briana.

'I'm going to show Briana where the drinks are.'

Nick was talking to Sally's boyfriend when she followed Sally to the table. Sally told her to choose something so she picked up a tall glass, filled it with a little Campari and topped it up with orange juice.

Sally gestured towards the others. 'Know anyone else?'

Briana shook her head. 'No-one, apart from Nick.'

'What do you think of him?'

There was no point in pretending. 'I like him, but we don't really see eye to eye.'

'Oh, really?' Sally tossed her shoulder-length blonde hair over her shoulders and looked intrigued. 'You and Nick haven't had much time to get to know one another, so what happened? Tell me more!'

'Oh . . . basically we agree to disagree about Phoebe and about Turtle Island — you know that Nick wants to buy it?'

'Yes, I've heard him say so, on and off for years, but I was never certain if he really meant it. Phoebe has managed her life, and that of Turtle Island, very well till now. Why shouldn't she carry on as she is for a while? She's all right, isn't she?'

'Oh, health-wise she's fine — but she's approaching eighty, and she's worried about the future. When Nick and I met the first time, I didn't like the way Nick talked about buying Turtle and taking it off her hands, as if there was no alternative.'

Sally looked puzzled and tilted her head to the side. 'Really? Nick is ambitious and determined perhaps, but he's never ruthless about people he cares about, and he likes Phoebe. She's become a kind of substitute grandmother.'

'That may be true, but I care about Phoebe too, and I've always thought of her as family. She was my gran's best friend; they went to boarding school together in England — and Gran would want me to take care of her now. That's what I'm trying to do.'

'So?' Sally waited; still puzzled.

Briana explained what she'd found out about friendly tourism. She told Sally what had to be done to get the proposal off the ground on Turtle Island, and what it might mean for Phoebe.

'Hmm! Sounds interesting. I've heard about schemes like that, but sometimes only the bored rich can afford that sort of location.'

'This time it would mean attracting people to Turtle who really care deeply about an intact environment for just a short visit. Hopefully it won't be too expensive and it certainly isn't intended to be a back-to-nature with every thinkable luxury thrown in.

'The island has so much going for it.

It's in the middle of a well-known vacation area, it's practically untouched by the banes of modern civilisation, it's fairly isolated and sparsely populated.'

Sally's eyes were drawn to a movement behind Briana's head for a moment, and she had an amused expression on her face. Briana wasn't surprised to find Nick was standing behind her, and had been listening intently.

The colour rose in her face. He moved around to face her, skimmed her features with dark, smooth eyes and said, 'Can I have a word with you?'

He caught her wrist, and pulled her gently but firmly away from Sally. Briana had no choice but to follow. Nick slowed his pace when they reached the edge of the group.

'Explain why you're rushing these plans through for Phoebe and Turtle Island.'

Briana shrugged before she went on determinedly. 'I'm not rushing, nothing has been finally decided. I'm only here for a short visit and if Phoebe decides to try the scheme out, it means I'll have to use my time effectively. My aim is to provide Phoebe with an additional source of income, that's all. I've done my homework about how feasible my idea is, and it does give her an alternative solution to selling. It's Phoebe's decision, I just want her to have a choice, that's all.'

He regarded her for a moment; they stared silently at each other in the half shadows. Briana looked over his head and saw the moon like a silver coin in the sky. Suddenly he gave her a smile. She blinked, and felt wary. His voice was deceivingly soft, and his eyes glinted dangerously. She was under no illusions when he said, 'So the swords are out, are they?'

Her mouth was dry; it was an effort to reply. 'Swords?'

'Aw, come off it! Of course you do!' He viewed her closely. The sea breezes were ruffling his shirt as he stood there looking devilishly handsome. 'The trouble with you, Briana, is that you are just naïve! You haven't thought about how your plans will really affect Phoebe, and haven't figured out the consequences for Turtle Island either!'

She struggled to maintain a conciliatory tone, although in the end the words came out in a rush. 'Perhaps your future plans will eventually change things even more than my idea of controlled tourism. My scheme means Phoebe can decide how many tourists she wants, and how often.' She ploughed on without censuring her words or thinking about the impression they made. 'At least I'm only thinking of Phoebe and the others on Turtle Island, and not just of myself!'

He just didn't understand why this girl from the other side of the Atlantic was so concerned about Turtle, or why she was getting under his skin either. He stared at her slightly baffled.

He ignored his fleeting thoughts and reminded himself if Phoebe wanted to sell, he'd buy; he wasn't going to justify himself, or get into a discussion with someone whose main aim since she arrived in the locality was to annoy him.

'You're so sure you know all the answers, don't you? Lady, believe me, you haven't a clue what you're getting yourself, or Phoebe, into!'

Briana bristled. 'And you do? If you have all the answers, why haven't you done something to push things along in the right direction before now?'

His voice was controlled and his eyes glittered in the sparse light from the moon. She was right, he should have done something before now to ease Phoebe's mind about the future, but there was no way he'd admit that to her at this moment. 'There's no point in spoiling the evening with pointless discussions. We'll agree to differ, shall we?'

He moved a few steps away and picked up a can of cold beer. The aluminium surface was misted and it was ice-cold in his hand. He gripped it so tight that it was already dented when he pulled the tab. It made a hissing sound and some of the liquid shot out and poured down the side, wetting his fingers, before he lifted it to his lips and took a long gulp. Wiping his lips with the back of his hand, he gave her a last glance, and then sauntered off to join some other people.

A few seconds later, when his anger began to fade, he wished he hadn't left her standing alone like that, but it was too late to back-pedal now.

Briana took a deep breath and stared up at the numerous stars twinkling in the sky. Clearly, he considered anything she did or said as a kind of personal provocation. He wasn't prepared to listen.

If Briana could find a feasible way to help her, she would; she owed that to her gran's lifelong friendship with Phoebe. Briana only hoped she could completely ignore the growing attraction she felt for Nick; even when they argued she felt a magnetism that she'd never experienced with anyone else before.

Sally watched them from a little way off. She didn't catch any of the conversation, but she could tell Nick was annoyed. She came to Briana's aid when Nick moved away.

Sally was diplomatic enough not to ask questions; she tucked her arm through Briana's and drew her back towards the others.

Briana positioned herself next to Sally and Brett near a bonfire of driftwood, where everyone was beginning to gather. She cradled her glass, and listened politely to strangers who talked about people and things that meant nothing to her. Nick had an attractive Chinese girl at his side and she felt jabs of envy and reminded herself that Nick Thornton was poison ivy, pleasant to look at, but fatal.

The salted wood sent bright sparks soaring into the sky, and the Chinese girl was hanging on his every word as well as his arm, and he did nothing to discourage her attention. Matt, a pilot with Zenith Air, ambled over to talk to Brett and Sally. Matt was friendly and eyed Briana's slim figure and attractive face with pleasure.

After her clash with Nick, it was bliss to bask in a man's attention. He asked her about her job, about herself, and her home. Briana concentrated on the pilot's voice and friendly eyes. Who needed Nick Thornton?

Nick tried to resist the temptation to watch Briana in the flickering light of the fire. Trouble was it was more difficult than he imagined; he liked women who weren't coy and didn't cling. Briana fitted both descriptions. He felt annoyed when he heard her laugh and looked across to see Matt at her side.

He realised that he'd never made her laugh. He shifted his weight and disentangled Li's arm when someone else caught her attention. Admittedly he hadn't improved things this evening; he'd been boorish and rude.

Trouble was, Briana had touched a sore point, and he didn't have himself under control!

Much later Briana went to look for Phoebe. Phoebe was still chatting to friends and acquaintances, and she seemed to be making the most of the evening. Briana didn't interrupt her and sat down on the nearby wall enjoying the sound of the ocean and the atmosphere. Matt found her there and invited her out for a meal the following week. Briana was pleased and accepted; she'd like to see him again.

It was nearly midnight when Phoebe joined Briana. She'd finally had enough and informed Briana that Nick was going to drive them back to the harbour. Briana nodded silently. He was doing Phoebe a favour, she just happened to be a hanger-on. They said thanks and goodbye to Nick's parents, and she followed Phoebe to Nick's car waiting in the driveway.

Without speaking, Briana squeezed herself on to the narrow back seat and arranged her legs at an angle. Phoebe sat next to Nick and they were soon busy chatting away. He drove them on to the quay where John was waiting. Phoebe thanked him and walked stiffly towards the quay steps an old-fashioned handbag over her arm.

Briana unfolded herself from the back seat, got out and said stiffly, 'Thank you for the lift, it was kind of you to bring us back.'

'No trouble.' His eyes eyed her languidly. 'Hope you enjoyed yourself.' He paused a second or two. 'I noticed Matt was taking good care of you.'

She coloured slightly and caught her breath. 'Yes, he's a very nice man! Just imagine, we even had a conversation for half-an-hour, and didn't argue once!'

She turned away, without waiting for his comment, but still heard the faint sound of Nick's choked laughter.

6

After Phoebe had opted to try the scheme, she told the other island inhabitants and they greeted the news with enthusiasm. They offered their support and help wherever it was needed. Briana wondered if they'd remembered all the other luckless schemes Phoebe had attempted in the past, but she found that they'd an unshakeable belief in Phoebe. She was the boss; any scheme of hers was worth trying.

Briana set the wheels in motion and they were lucky. The agencies' addresses she'd been given in the UK and the States agreed to put them on their list of last minute offers. They'd caught the attention of some people looking for alternative destinations. The first guests would arrive in two weeks, and everything had to be ready by then.

Briana spent the coolest part of each day doing as much as she could. It was almost eleven o'clock now, and Briana was still on her knees with sweat pouring out of every pore sanding-down one of the floors.

John, Robert and Terry helped with the physical work whenever they could, and the women rallied round to make curtains and matching bedspreads, and by scouting for low-cost furniture on Windblown.

Briana was doing her best to continue with sanding the floors prior to sealing them with wax. The men would have worked faster, but the path to the lagoon was very important too. It would keep visitors from using Phoebe's access. Thinking of the sanding work still to be done on this hut and the other two huts, Briana dabbled with the idea of hiring a sanding machine, but it was just an extra expense.

Phoebe had no money reserves, and some kind of financing was needed to get the project off the ground, so Briana invested most of her remaining savings.

Briana hadn't heard or seen anything of Nick since the night of the barbecue. She'd gone out with Matt, the pilot she met at the barbecue, twice. They'd gone for a meal at a local restaurant, and then he took her to a bar where a steel band made wonderful music that sent her feet tapping. Last weekend, she spent Sunday with him on Windblown. They visited a beach, spending the day enjoying each other's company and the wonderful surroundings.

She was on all fours rubbing at the surface with the block; her skin glistening with perspiration, her clothes, hair and body covered in sawdust and dirt. Briana was unaware of him till she heard Nick's amused voice somewhere behind her.

'Hi! What a wonderful advert for sandpaper or a sawmill!'

She jumped. Colour flooded her face as she recognised his voice, looked around and saw him. 'Oh! It's you! You gave me a fright creeping up like that.'

'Did I? Not intentional, I assure you!'

Briana scrambled awkwardly to her feet; extremely conscious of how she looked. She was wearing an old pair of Phoebe's shorts held up by some thick cord through the tabs.

'He seemed to be enjoying the situation and sounded very matter-of-fact. 'I called to see Phoebe. She told me you were here. I decided to come and see what you're doing.'

Briana thrust the sandpaper-block at him. 'I don't need spectators! You can help, if you like.'

A dark eyebrow raised in amusement. He looked around. 'You're sandpapering the floors? By hand? Good heavens! How far have you got?'

Mesmerised by his eyes, she tried to get her emotions under control. Somehow he always managed to set her pulse racing.

'One hut is finished. I started this today. Then there are two more.'

'Where are the men, why can't they do this?' His expression darkened with an unreadable emotion.

'They're all working hard and help all the time! John has a full-time job and spends every free minute working here! They're cutting a path to the beach today; when they're finished, they'll come back and help me here.'

He sighed with exasperation. 'You know that I think this is a mad scheme, but why not use a sanding machine?'

She looked at him in surprise. She'd expected only criticism and censure, not suggestions. 'There's no electricity here, and anyway . . . hiring a machine costs money. Money we need badly for other things.'

He moved unexpectedly forward and brushed some sawdust from her cheek.

'Don't let any chivalrous instincts mislead you. I started this, I'm responsible, and I'll finish it!' she said.

'You're just being pig-headed and obstinate!'

'I must say it's always a joy to see you, Nick; you constantly say such nice things to me, don't you?'

95

He stared at her and then burst out laughing. 'Sorry! You're right, of course; it's none of my business. I realise that I'm not a very diplomatic person when you're around — perhaps because I know you give as good as you get.'

She gave a soft chuckle. 'You find it much easier to handle docile and easily persuaded women, don't you? But it's better for you not to get your own way all the time!'

His eyes closed slightly and his lips twitched. 'You're just trying to justify your ... how shall I put it ... ? Straightforward manner! Truth is you're just determined, like me.'

Briana smiled and shook her head. She was glad that even though they couldn't always agree on what was right for Phoebe, they could still communicate on the same wavelength. Briana was glad to find that he wasn't completely intolerant.

He looked at his watch. 'I'll leave you to it. Phoebe told me to tell you it was time to come home because it's too hot, and I agree — you should take a break!'

She nodded drinking in details of his face. 'I was about to finish anyway. For your information, I never work in the heat of the afternoon.'

He turned on his heel and lifted his hand silently in farewell.

Briana sighed softly, still confused by his unexpected appearance.

Nick quickened his pace through the vegetation. His canvas shoes made no sound and he was alone with his thoughts as he made his way back to the yacht.

Briana was tired after the morning's work; she slept a dreamless sleep as soon as her head hit the pillow. Two hours later she finished her refreshing break with Phoebe on the veranda with fruit and lots of juice before her thoughts turned to the waiting work.

'I'll be off, Phoebe. With a little luck the second hut might be finished by tonight.'

Phoebe looked at her. 'I feel really

bad about all the work you're putting in, Briana.'

Briana patted her veined hand covered in age-spots reassuringly. 'I'm enjoying myself in an odd sort of way!' She smiled reassuringly.

'Well, that doesn't make me feel better. Sometimes I wish I hadn't agreed to this scheme now.' Phoebe looked at Briana with an appealing expression. 'The older you get, the more you worry about everything.'

Briana smiled knowingly. 'Yes, I know. Don't worry; Gran was the same. She worried that the milkman was seriously ill if the milk wasn't delivered on time, and daft things like that all the time.' Briana rose, stretching as she did so. 'I'll be back as soon as the light begins to fade.'

'Hmm. I'll have a meal ready; at least I'll make sure you're fed properly!'

Briana didn't admit to Phoebe she felt daunted by the thought of all the sanding work still waiting. She threw back her shoulders. Thinking about work didn't get it done!

There was a faint buzzing sound as she approached the huts. It grew louder as she got closer. She pushed open the door; the usual creaking noise it made was lost in the din. She was amazed to find the floor she'd begun that morning was already smooth and blank.

A quick glance into the room that used to be the kitchen showed her that was also finished. She moved towards the bedroom, where the sound came from, and pushed the door tentatively open.

Nick was kneeling on the floor with a machine in his hands, and thick white dust coated everything. He spotted her out of the corner of his eye, looked up, and then shut off the machine before he stood up. His mouth was covered by a facemask, and he pulled it off.

'What on earth . . . ?' Briana was so surprised that she was lost for words.

They exchanged a long deep look. He quipped, 'I thought you might melt away in the sun if you didn't get some mechanical help.'

The relief that he'd finished most of this hut already was coupled with the incredible realisation that Nick, of all people, was helping her. He was hostile to the whole scheme and the last person she expected to help. 'I . . . I'm flabbergasted!' She looked around. 'This is absolutely wonderful. But you need electricity . . . ?'

He shook his head and lifted the sander. 'Battery driven machines.' He explained. 'Only trouble is they have to be recharged and that takes time. There's enough power to finish this hut, but then the batteries will need recharging to do the next.'

'Where did you get a machine?'

'Have one on board! There are often sanding jobs to do on board ships.'

'Considering you think that I'm slightly mad, you are being very kind. You've saved me days of work already — but this is my baby not yours! Let me take over — that's if you trust me to use your machine.'

He held out the machine with good humour. 'Of course, but I like to finish what I start, and I'll finish this. I'll give you quick instructions on how to use it, so that you can attack the next hut tomorrow morning. You can recharge the batteries overnight back at the house.'

'I brought you a mask too, it's over there on the window-sill. Come here! I'll show you what you have to do, give you a chance to practise, and then I'll carry on. I'll go and get something to drink from Phoebe; this is thirsty work and there's nothing here — I've looked.' His dark eyes had amusement buried in their depths.

She didn't understand why he was being so helpful, and he didn't explain. She walked across to him, and he handed her the machine. It was lighter than she expected.

Briana got down on her knees. She pressed the starting button and vibrations slid up her arms as she moved it back and forth.

He watched her efforts silently from above for a few moments. 'There's no need to put all your weight on it like that. Just hold it firmly and move it steadily across the surface. Remember to keep it away from any clothes, and punch the safety button there — the red one — if you're in trouble.' His tone of voice was warm. 'Here! Let me!'

She swallowed tightly as he dropped to one knee; she glanced up into his face and wished her heart would behave. His warm breath fanned her cheek and she felt mesmerised. His arms encircled her shoulders, trapping her in the inner curve of his body. Placing his hands on top of hers holding the machine, he guided it evenly. Her body tingled from the contact, and she had no desire to move away.

After a few moments he let go and got to his feet again. It was hard to remain coherent; Briana's mind was spinning with bewilderment at the effect he was having on her.

Nick straightened. 'I'll leave you for a couple of minutes; to give you a chance to get used to it. I'll get that drink. Back soon!'

Briana nodded and returned her attention to the sanding. By the time he came back she was covered in a film of fine dust. He was tempted to laugh, but he kept himself under control. He held out his hand and helped her to her feet. He took the sanding machine off her, and went to work on the section that wasn't finished yet.

'What am I supposed to do?' she asked.

He answered indulgently. 'Go for a swim! I'll finish the hut, and you can carry on tomorrow.'

Briana watched the muscles working under his shirt. 'I'm terribly grateful for what you're doing Nick, you've saved me days and days of hard work.'

He nodded to the floor in front of him. 'Tell you what, I'll come back on Sunday, and if you like we'll go for a sail round the islands. Ask Phoebe if she'd like to come. Would you like to come?'

Briana hoped she looked a lot calmer than she felt. 'I . . . I . . . Yes.'

He looked satisfied. 'Good. I'll get here early.'

She wanted to contribute something. 'I'll bring something to eat and drink — a kind of picnic lunch if you like.'

He smiled without answering. 'I'll come up to the house for you, and Phoebe, if she decides to come.'

She smiled and nodded. She had to restrain from whooping with pleasure when she was out of sight of the huts and on her way back to Phoebe's. She sighed with pleasure at the thought of the turquoise water, and white sand as she shouldered her towel.

As Nick had imagined, Phoebe didn't want to come.

She'd answered. 'You'd need a crane to get me up the rope ladder . . . no, no! My days of gadding about are over.' Secretly Phoebe eyed Briana and hoped that the two of them would learn to enjoy each other's company.

Nick was very relaxed and pleased with himself when he arrived. He wore close-fitting dark blue slacks and a white polo shirt; he looked like a very attractive sea-wolf. Briana had already packed a small wicker basket with cold chicken, salad, fruit, cake, juice and a bottle of white wine. She'd donned a swimsuit under white slacks and a black and white T-shirt. 'Hi. You're punctual!'

He chatted to Phoebe for a few minutes and accepted a fruit juice. Phoebe shooed them off, and although neither of them said anything, they had no regrets about leaving Phoebe on her own for once. When they reached the yacht, he held out his hand to steady her as she climbed the rope ladder to the deck. To Briana's untrained eye it seemed very big.

'Gosh, close up it's very impressive!' Briana steadied herself.

'Take the basket below.' He pointed down some shallow steps. 'There's a small galley with a fridge. Have a look around. We'll leave straight away.'

'I don't know a thing about sailing, but if you think I can help, you only have to say so.'

His expression softened. 'I'll use the engine until we get out beyond the main reef, and if the wind is good enough I'll put you at the helm while I run the sails.'

'Are you properly insured?' she asked.

He grinned, and she went below. She was glad to get away from his sight for a couple of minutes to calm her thoughts. She glanced around at the beautiful high-gloss woodwork and dark blue fittings. If she could keep her emotions under control, it would be a day to remember.

It was. The water got choppier and the waves bigger, but Briana found it was quite exhilarating to travel across the surface of the water at speed like a sea-bird, and she watched how Nick kept the boat on course. It was easy to laugh and just enjoy the day; time passed quickly.

He stopped eventually at a small, uninhabited island. Nick anchored and stretched his long body towards the sun in contentment as he divested himself of his outer clothes and dived neatly overboard. Briana followed his lead and joined him.

On shore she sauntered along at his side as they circled the island on foot. It was no effort to keep a string of various topics going. Briana mused that they were on the same wavelength about so many things; it was a pity his attitude about Turtle Island was such a stumbling block.

Briana wandered happily at his side. Her emotions were at an all time high. They swam back to the yacht and shared the picnic. The salty air and the exercise had made them both hungry; hunger satisfied, they sipped some of the cold white wine and Briana leaned back contentedly in the cushioning, lifting her face to the sun.

'Thanks for today, Nick. This is just wonderful!' He gave her an answering broad smile and her pulse accelerated. 'Will you try ship-chartering one day, after all? Phoebe told me you planned to do so, and then Darren was killed and you put it aside.'

He shrugged. 'I'm not sure if I want to do it for a living any more. At the time I thought it would be an excellent way of getting my own yacht, and being able to sail as much as I wanted — but I've achieved that in a roundabout way too.'

'Tell me to mind my own business if I'm being too inquisitive, but could you just get up and leave the airline to do something else if you wanted to? I get the impression the rest of the family take it for granted that you'll stay and work there for as long as Zenith flies?'

'I suppose they do. Zenith would need someone to run it properly if I did — and a good executive would demand a high wage and reduce the profits — but it'd be possible. The airline is family owned, and all of us get more income from the shares they own, than from their earnings as employees. On the other hand, if we do hit hard times, we're also prepared to do without for the sake of the future.' He twisted the stem of his glass in his large brown hands. 'Anyway, I owe it to my brother to keep things afloat until his kids have finished their education and can fend for themselves.'

Briana looked at him carefully. 'I can understand why you feel that way, but you've loaded an awful lot on your shoulders, haven't you?'

'You make it sound like a dramatic decision; it wasn't. Darren would have done the same for me in the same circumstance, and I don't see it as a burden. Zenith gives the family a decent income, and if I did decide to put my engines into something else, I still hope that Zenith will continue to make money.'

'I realise that, but if you wanted to passionately do something else it isn't fair to be nailed down just because your brother died and left a widow and children. Perhaps you'll see things differently when you have a wife and family of your own?'

He was leaning on the railway opposite Briana, and he shifted his position. 'I've no intention of marrying. When I remember how Darren's death affected us all, and left Sally to bring up two children on her own — I don't want to leave someone to face the same problem as she had.'

'Don't you like children?'

He lifted his shoulder. 'Yeah, I like children, they're sometimes a lot more fun than adults. I haven't given serious thought on having any myself, because they just wouldn't fit my lifestyle.'

'Darren's death was a cruel touch of fate; and it seems to have altered your whole way of life in more ways than one.' It was a statement that called for a comment.

He stared over her head out to sea. 'He was my twin brother, we were inseparable up until he married, and even then we were very close. When he died, a part of me died with him. I still can't believe it.'

She answered softly. 'Life isn't always fair is it? You ask yourself why it happened to you and not to someone else, but there is no answer. You just have to carry on.' She clasped her hands tightly together. 'When my mother died I was eight. The memories of her are anchored in my brain, and I still miss her. My whole life fell to pieces when she died and left me.

'I was even mad at her for leaving me behind. I felt deserted and cheated, and I wished I was dead too. I eventually found a haven with my gran and she gave me all the love she could.' Briana paused and he nodded sympathetically. 'I turned to my gran, perhaps it would have been better for you if you'd had someone to turn to — I suspect you didn't though, did you?'

He shook his head a little. 'My parents and Sally needed my support, I didn't think much about my own feelings at the time.'

'You reject the idea of getting married because of some hypothetical idea that you'll get killed and have to leave your family to look after themselves, but you shouldn't. If I reacted in the same way I'd never want to have children because I'd be afraid of dying and leaving them — but I love children, and I'd love some of my own. You have to trust in fate. We don't understand all that happens to us, but perhaps we're not meant to!'

He got up and threw the remains of his wine into the sea. He looked down at her. 'You haven't had a very easy time of it, have you?'

'My gran was wonderful. She compensated for as much as she could, and I managed to cope with the rest.'

He viewed her speculatively. 'I think you've muddled through very well, and you came out of it on top; I'm sure your mother would have been proud of the way you turned out. Where was your father when all this happened?'

She shrugged and tilted her head to

the side. 'He was coping with his own grief. He wanted to help me, and tried to keep the two of us together, but he was a salesman with a big company. He had to go away for days at a time, so in the end I was spending so much time with my gran it became a permanent situation because of my schooling. A couple of years later, Dad remarried, and he and Marcia, his new wife, tried hard to integrate me into their new family. Marcia has two girls of her own; we were roughly the same age and can you imagine the arguments and friction between three teenage girls!'

He laughed softly. 'I've seen how you can fight for what you believe in, so I can imagine the fur flew in all directions!'

She pretended to ignore the inference and continued. 'In the end everyone, including Dad, Marcia, Gran and me decided it was the best solution for me to go back to Gran permanently. I was happy from then on — it really was the best solution for us all.'

He studied her face and nodded. 'You have a strange affect on me, Briana. You've had a hard time of it and come through with flags flying and it hasn't made you scared to face the future, has it? In fact it's brought out your fighting qualities.' He grinned briefly and then grew silent. 'I can't remember ever talking to anyone about how I felt about Darren's death.'

Briana smiled at him. 'You can pretend in front of others for a long time, but one day it all falls away and you look in the mirror and you realise you are alone. If you can share the sadness with someone who understands, I think you can get through life much easier — even though it still hurts and it's a long and lonely process.'

'I didn't want to burden my parents in that way, because I thought it would make things worse, but perhaps you're right. I suppose they were supporting each other through it all.'

'Probably! I hope you don't ignore the subject of your brother with them; it will hurt them more if they think you don't mention Darren's name because you've forgotten him!'

He looked thoughtful and rubbed his chin. 'You may be right! And no-one has ever asked me. Everyone just took it for granted that I'd digested it all.'

Her heart skipped a beat. 'It's not my job to pry, analyse or comment on your life, I'm only telling you how I coped! I should mind my own business.'

He held her glance and shook his head. 'I think you seem to like helping others, and that's not a bad characteristic by my sense of reckoning!'

She flushed a little. 'Gosh! For heaven's sake, Nick! Don't say anything nice to me, or I'll never recover from the shock.'

He grinned. 'That would be fatal wouldn't it? We haven't clashed today, not once let's keep it that way.' He looked at his watch. 'We'll have to turn back to Turtle now. I've a business meeting this evening.'

Briana was sorry the outing was

coming to an end. She understood completely why women found him so attractive. They sailed into the lagoon. He helped her down the rope ladder into the dingy, rowed her to shore, and handed her the wicker basket. He tilted his cap and looked down at her, a tender smile spread across his face and his eyes were warm and friendly.

Unexpectedly he bent his head and kissed her gently on her lips without a word. It was a feather-like touch, and lacked any deep emotion, but for Briana it was enough to wish it could go on, and that he'd kiss her with passion. He didn't of course; he turned back to the dingy and pushed off.

7

Briana was deep in the criminal happenings of her paperback story and didn't pay much attention to the conversation as the two age-old friends chatted. A couple of minutes later Phoebe returned the phone to its cradle and stated, 'That was Mary!'

Briana nodded absentmindedly. 'Yes, so I gather!'

Phoebe chuckled. 'She's been arguing with the local minister again, just because he won't consider moving the service forward an hour on a Sunday evening: she wants to watch that detective series, and the times clash. She's just come back from a church meeting.'

Briana looked up and grinned.

'She saw Nick on the way home.'

'Did she?'

'Out . . . with that assistant of his.

They were going into that swanky restaurant that's just opened on Gibbs Street. I sometimes wonder if he's getting serious at last. I noticed them together at the barbeque. Are they really just boss and employee! You met her, didn't you? What's she like?'

The smile on her face faded and Briana swallowed hard. Nick said he had a business meeting; perhaps that's just a cover up, because he didn't want to tell her about his private life?

'She's beautiful; shoulder-length black shiny hair, huge almond-shaped eyes, perfect skin and delicate bone structure.'

'Hmph! Looks aren't everything in this life. I hope she deserves him if he's getting interested.' Phoebe put a hand behind her, to support the small of her back, and sighed softly. 'My back is playing up again. I think I'll go and have a bath and an early night.'

'Do that!' Briana tried to repeat the smile, and turned her attention back to her paperback. The print swam in an unrecognisable blur as her thoughts circled and dodged about. It was none of her business what Nick did, or with whom.

Unseen by Briana, Phoebe looked back thoughtfully from the doorway as her thoughts wandered. Phoebe studied Briana's expression before she went out to the hall. She grasped the banister to help her on the way upstairs.

All next day Briana noticed that the weather was changing. It was oppressively hot, much too hot and it was also too sultry. Phoebe complained after breakfast about feeling tired and listless, and forecasted that a storm was on its way. She was right. As the day progressed Briana could see, by the changing colour of the sky, that something unusual was about to happen.

The wind increased steadily, sending slate grey clouds speeding across the sky like flying carpets. It bent the trunks of the palm trees back and forth like drinking straws with hats on, and the palm leaves gyrated about in agony in the wild currents of air. Just before the thunder and lightning shattered the serenity of the island, the daylight finally faded into an eerie darkness. The ferocious claps of thunder were louder than anything Briana had experienced, and although she ventured out on to the balcony to see what was going on, she was glad to return to the safety of the living room.

Phoebe was flipping through a magazine.

Briana tidied her windswept hair with her hands. 'Gosh, Phoebe! Does it get any worse?'

Phoebe looked at her, over the rim of her glasses. 'Hard to say. The storm seems to be peaking at the moment, and apart from a bit of damage to the vegetation, we should be all right. A hurricane would be more unpleasant, believe me.'

The fact that Phoebe found it all perfectly normal, helped Briana; in the end she was so engrossed in her story that she didn't notice the storm had receded and splashes of gold and red colour had replaced the dismal greys and sombre blacks again. The storm had moved on to another target.

Phoebe came back in from surveying things from the veranda. 'Briana, the storm's passed by. Let's see how much damage it's caused in the village. I always worry about them; those huts are pretty fragile and I'm scared something awful will happen one day. I wish I had money to build them solid houses.'

Briana dropped her book on the table, and got up quickly. 'Yes, that's a good idea!'

There were dozens of ripped palm leaves and remains of other vegetation lying haphazardly around as they made their way, but the villagers were already busy clearing the debris near their huts. Phoebe was clearly relieved nothing too bad had happened and chatted to everyone before she made the trip back to her bungalow again. By the time they got back, Phoebe was glad to sit down on the veranda.

Briana left her there and set out again to follow a circular path that meandered around the periphery of the whole island. It snaked past the mangroves, along some very rocky coastline, and then took a short detour inland to its highest point. From there Briana had a view of the whole island. The sea was still stormy, but the sky was clear and the sun was breaking through again.

The air was fresh and clean again and it was time to think about the evening meal. They were busy preparing it when Mary phoned to check how Phoebe was. Briana heard them chatting as she continued to clean the vegetables for their meal.

Phoebe came back with a worried look on her face. 'Hmm! I hope Nick's all right.'

Briana continued to de-seed a bright red pepper. 'What about?'

'Mary's next door neighbour, Bill,

just came back from the harbour and heard that Nick took his yacht out just before the storm started, and no-one has been able to contact him since, although he does have a radio on board. How could he be so idiotic! He knows how violent storms can be at this time of the year, why did he choose to go out this afternoon of all times?'

Briana's stomach did a somersault, and the pepper slid from her fingers into the basin. The picture of Nick fighting the storm in the middle of a turbulent ocean sent her thoughts haywire. 'He'll be all right, won't he?'

Phoebe noted the anxiety in Briana's voice. Phoebe was worried herself, but she was surprised by the depth of Briana's concern. She seemed to be unnecessarily concerned about a man whom she spent most of her time quarrelling with. Phoebe tried to reassure her; there was no point in both of them worrying. 'Nick knows the sea like the back of his hand, and his boat is equipped to cope with worse storms than today's.'

Briana picked up the pepper again and began to chop it with hands that still weren't properly under control. In just a few weeks he'd got under her skin, and taken possession of her heart. She had fallen in love with Nicolas Thornton. He wasn't the kind of man she hoped to fall in love with; her brain told her he was the wrong kind of man, but her heart told her he was right.

She tried to remain calm; she couldn't leave the kitchen, not without a good excuse. Phoebe would think it strange if she dashed off leaving her alone to finish the preparations for the evening meal — they'd always shared the work, ever since she'd arrived.

Briana spent a sleepless night. In the end she gave up and slipped out in the middle of the night to go down to the beach. He had to be safe! She dare not think anything else, not for a single moment.

The morning air was beautifully clean and fresh as they took their frugal breakfast on the veranda. Briana's hand gripping her coffee mug jumped when the phone rang. She tried to listen from afar as Phoebe talked to Mary.

A short time later Phoebe put down the receiver and joined her again. Briana took a deep breath and viewed her nervously.

'Nick's safe! He anchored in one of the outlying islands, and waited till the storm was over. He sailed back at first light this morning.'

Briana felt so much relief she was glad she was sitting; otherwise her knees might have given way. It was like having a lead cloak lifted from her heart. She looked down quickly, so that Phoebe couldn't see her expression. Phoebe wasn't stupid and she didn't need to be a fortune-teller to notice something unusual was going on. Briana had been quiet since last night, and her eyes had been full of apprehension all day.

Once Briana had absorbed the news, her feelings spiralled rapidly upwards.

Buoyed up by the relief of knowing he was safe and unharmed, she announced she was off to check if the tourist huts had been badly damaged. The first visitors were arriving in a couple of days; if there were repairs, they had to be done fast.

Briana was glad to sit back and relax. She'd been very busy the last couple of days; helping the others to clear up the storm damage, and putting the finishing touches to the huts. Perhaps the tourists would anticipate something different; she had no idea of what people expected to find when they visited an *unspoiled* island.

When they arrived, all of them seemed delighted with their surroundings, and with their lodgings. It was another weight off her mind.

Briana had kept Phoebe out of things as far as she could. She knew that Phoebe was worried whether everything would work out, and probably also worried about how much the goings-on would intrude on her day-to-day life.

She'd never admit that to Briana of course. Briana noticed that apart from going down to the huts with Briana for a couple of minutes to meet the people on the day after their arrival, Phoebe had blended into the background.

She clearly didn't want to be drawn in on the organisation or the running of the scheme — and it made Briana wonder if her idea was such a good one after all. Tourists wanted to be left to their own devices, but they needed someone to turn to if problems cropped up. Briana decided that she'd have to get the villagers to take over welcoming, settling, and looking after the people. They were all naturally hospitable and helpful people, and they cared about Phoebe; Briana was also sure that a small wage for handling everything would also be welcome.

Briana was satisfied and enjoying the cool of the evening on the veranda with a glass of cold fruit juice and her own thoughts. Phoebe had pleaded tiredness and had left her after the evening meal.

Briana wondered if something special was bothering her. It wasn't like Phoebe to go to bed early, and she'd disappeared early the last couple of days.

Briana twisted the glass in her hand, stared into the distance and decided to mention it to Mary next time she had a chance. Mary knew Phoebe best of all, and could judge if it was a bad sign or not.

Briana let the rocker move gently to and fro as her thoughts wandered back and forth in the fading daylight. She tried to remind herself that Phoebe was nearly eighty; it was natural for her to get tired. Briana hadn't had much time to think about anyone or anything, not even about Nick.

She still didn't know how she'd react when they met again. She was just another woman to him, no-one special, just Phoebe's visitor from the UK. If she kept reminding herself of that fact, she might be able to keep her thoughts to herself, and disappear again without making a fool of herself. She'd be gone in a couple of weeks, and it was quite likely she'd never see him again.

A few days later, after they just had their evening meal, Phoebe handed her the phone and told her Nick wanted to talk to her. As she picked up the receiver, her heart skipped and then it beat so loudly, she felt he must be able to hear it. Her voice faltered; she cleared her throat. The words still came out with a squeak. 'Nick?'

'Hi, if you're not doing anything special, I wondered if you'd like to come out? Some of us are going to the *Hideaway*. It's a local eating-place with a bar and a small disco. I thought you might like a little more action and a change of scenery?'

At the sound of his voice, her hand went up to her throat. Briana was glad he couldn't see the confusion in her eyes. She tried to sound nonchalant, while trying to quell the excitement. She pushed the knowledge of his other meetings, with other women, to the back of her mind. He was asking her,

129

and not someone else. 'Umm . . . Yes, I'd like to.'

His voice had an audible edge of amusement; she could imagine the slight upturn of his lips and the sparkle in his eyes. 'You know me, Briana; always the gentleman!'

She felt light-headed. 'No comment! Where do we meet?'

'Ask John to ferry you across. I'll pick you up at the pier at 7.30, OK?'

She nodded, although he couldn't see her. 'What time will I be coming back? I'll have to ask him to pick me up.'

'Oh . . . not before twelve I should imagine.'

She felt the disappointment rising. 'Then perhaps I'd better not come.' Her heart sank and she bit her lip in dismay. 'I can't expect John to stay up late just for me. It was different when Phoebe and I came to your parents' barbeque. That was on a Saturday so I didn't feel so bad about asking him — but he has to get up early every day, for work. It wouldn't be fair.' Resignedly she said. 'Thanks for asking anyway.'

There was a moment of silence. 'Look — I'll tell my mother you're going to stay with them overnight. Then you can go back with John tomorrow afternoon.'

She was startled. 'You . . . you can't just dump me on your parents overnight!'

'My mother won't mind. It's no problem; their guest room is always ready. She's very flexible and hospitable; it won't bother her, promise! Don't fuss, girl, just come.' There was a click and the phone was dead again.

She was uneasy; but on the other hand the thought of being able to see him again dissolved her misgivings.

Briana made haste. She looked at her watch, she didn't have time to wash her hair, but she'd have a shower and change into something fresh. Less than half-an-hour later, she slipped a pale-green, body-skimming dress with spaghetti shoulder straps over her head.

The hem skimmed her knees, and showed off her tanned legs. Not bad! She brushed her hair until it shone, but as ever she was sparing with make-up.

Throwing a T-shirt, cotton trousers and some overnight things quickly into a small holdall, she rushed downstairs, out into the darkness and down the path to the village. Luckily John and his family had just finished their evening meal, and he broke into a broad smile as she explained what she wanted. They neared the quay in Liberty, barely a quarter-of-an-hour later. There was no-one waiting, but Briana knew she was early.

She arranged to meet John next afternoon and waved him off. Glad to have got there on time, she settled down on the rough stonewall bordering the quayside.

It was only a matter of minutes until she saw his car. He sounded the horn as the red convertible drew level, and she got up expectantly, a smile spread across her face and her eyes were alight with expectation. Inside her head, the smile faded when she noticed there were other people in the car, although it was still frozen to her lips.

Next to him, in the passenger seat with the Chinese girl, Li. He got out; his tall figure towered above her and he reached out to take her holdall. He tipped his seat forward and held the door open, so that she could squeeze into the back, to sit next to a man she'd never seen before. Getting into the driving seat, Nick introduced him as Garry Miles, and nodded in the direction of Li, with the remark 'you already know each other'.

Briana caught his eye in the mirror, nodded, and gave him as genuine a smile as she could manage. She looked out of the window as the car picked up speed, she swallowed her disappointment and listened to the others chatting.

Briana pulled herself together and listened to them as they told her about the *Hideaway*. She nodded to no-one in particular in the dark, and was glad the shadows hid her face. For some stupid reason she'd assumed she'd be alone with Nick. Trying to control her disappointment, she sat in lonely silence.

They drove for several minutes along the coast before Nick turned off down a road towards a large bungalow-shaped building close to the sea. It was surrounded by tropical greenery and had a large terrace, where coloured hanging lamps and flickering candle-light produced a romantic effect. They got out, and Briana was careful not to stumble in the process; she wanted to avoid his touch.

A lot of people were enjoying an evening meal on the terrace as they moved indoors towards music, laughter and subdued lighting in the bar. She'd time to reorganise her thoughts; she thrust back her shoulders as she kept pace with the others. She was deter-mined he'd never find out that she'd fallen in love with him, or that he'd become the centre of everything she'd always desired.

She made no special effort to gain his attention. Every time his gaze met hers, her heart turned over in response, but she looked elsewhere. She couldn't avoid noticing how much attention he got from Li, nor did she miss his bantering replies and soft laughter.

The bar was beginning to fill up and Briana was glad she could use the cover of the crowd to seem happy and relaxed. Everyone seemed to know each other, and Briana made an effort to blend in with them all. If her smiles were artificial, no-one noticed. Some of them gradually drifted towards the small dance floor and Briana joined them; she needed to get away from Nick and she wanted to be alone with her own thoughts.

She'd always enjoyed dancing. Her Gran had sent her to ballroom dancing lessons in the next town when she was fifteen, and although she'd protested that it was old-fashioned and a waste of time, in the end Briana actually enjoyed it.

Briana mingled and tried to lose herself in moving to the music. Gradually it helped to eradicate the feeling of disenchantment a little. If she didn't think of Nick all the time, it wouldn't hurt quite as much.

The sound blaring from the loudspeakers was a mixture of popular music. Suddenly Nick was standing nearby, and as he put down his glass and took her hand, some slow, romantic music filled the air. Short of actually pushing him away, she had no choice.

'You seem to be enjoying yourself?' He pulled her into his arms and she felt crushed against his chest. Putting a large hand on the small of her back, he seemed to draw her even closer. Blood pounded through her brain, and her knees felt they were on the brink of giving way. She held on and tried to sound detached.

'Umm! It's nice here.' She was glad the subdued lighting hid her flushed cheeks. Her head rested on his chest beneath his chin, and she concentrated on breathing and staying alive. The music bound their bodies together. Her mind told her to resist the feeling of pleasure, but her body refused to listen. She had to distract herself with some kind of conversation.

'I hear you almost got yourself into big trouble the other day — with your yacht?'

He shook his head. 'No trouble. I misjudged how quickly the storm would reach us, but I was never in danger. I'm not stupid enough to take unnecessary risks, Briana!'

She adopted the expression she used for disobedient pupils. 'I hope so. We were all very worried about you.'

'Were you? I feel suitably honoured!' His voice had a teasing quality, and she coloured. Watching her intently, he changed the subject. 'Actually, I wondered if this was your kind of thing! I thought that environmental angels like you might find a discotheque decadent, useless, and all that!'

She replied with as much buoyancy as she could muster. 'I care about the world, it doesn't mean I don't like enjoying myself. It is possible to do both, you know!'

He gave a soft laugh, and her pulse increased. She breathed in his after-shave or soap, or deodorant — whatever it was, it was attractive without being over-powering. He held her in his arms and they moved in perfect unison around the small dance floor. He danced surprisingly well, and she stored the memory. He was quietly concentrating and so was she, and the movement of his body guiding hers, gave her a feeling of perfect contentment for a few minutes. It seemed like seconds, but it could have been minutes or hours, when the music stopped. He looked down and grinned, before he released her. He forced her to turn a pirouette before faster music filled the air again.

Looking at her intently, he asked,

'Staying here, or joining us over at the bar?'

Briana didn't like to muse who 'us' were. It was safer not to get too involved with him. She tried a smile, and plastered it stiffly to her face. 'I'll join you in a few minutes!'

He nodded and turned away. She watched him go, and wondered why people often fell in love with the wrong person. After dancing out her frustration alone, for a while, she slipped out through the crowd, out across the emptying terrace, and down to the beach where she headed for a comfortable dark spot under a palm tree.

The waves hitting the beach, crashed softly into the night. The sounds and the scene helped her to calm her thoughts; this was something good for her to remember for the rest of her life.

She didn't know how long she'd been there; it seemed quite a while, but it wasn't. The sound of footsteps on the loose gravel leading down to the beach brought her back to earth. Before she even turned around to look who it was as he slipped on the coral sand to join her, she knew it was Nick.

He reached her; and had a teasing sound to his voice as he said, 'So, this is where you are? No-one knew where you'd gone, so I came looking.'

She stared up at him without replying. He held out his hand, and she took it. Once she was on her feet, she studied the lean face, and his nearness made her senses spin again. She looked down quickly, and brushed her dress free of sand. 'It's fantastic here; the sea, the sky, the smells. I was just wishing I could store it away in a bottle, so that I am able to uncork it one day a long time from now. I'll remember it for the rest of my life. You take it all for granted but it's a dream.'

'Apart from the occasional storm we get, I'm inclined to agree with you — it's a great place to live.' He was so close she could feel the heat from his body, and her heart lurched madly. The wind was playing with his hair. He put a finger under her chin and lifted her face a little. When he bent his head and kissed her, she had no time to get her instincts fully under control.

Her response to him was overpowering, Briana had an urge to kiss him back, but somehow she mustered enough self-control not to give herself completely away, her communication skills had disappeared. He was the one who finally broke the silence.

'Let's get back to the others. Li and Garry are waiting to leave; it's a working day for us all tomorrow.' His arms dropped to his side again. He studied her tawny eyes; they were black and unfathomable in the semi-darkness. The sea breezes plastered her flimsy dress to her body and he remembered how it felt to hold her.

Briana's thoughts were still spinning and she fought to control her emotions. 'Oh . . . Yes, of course! Sorry!' She tried a weak smile. 'You forget that others have a job to do when you're on holiday.'

'You're forgiven!' He took her hand

and led her up the beach. His hand felt warm, comforting and right.

She longed to reach up and touch where his lips had been. He released her hand when they reached the terrace. Briana didn't know whether to be glad or sorry. She just followed his lead and tried not to get things out of proportion; a kiss meant next to nothing these days.

Li and Garry were waiting in the bar. She had no time to mull over the situation anyway — they piled into Nick's car again after a bit of bantering and drove off. Only minutes later he drew up in front of his parents' bungalow. The other two waited for him as he grabbed her bag from the boot and took her to the door. He opened it with one of his keys, and went ahead of her towards the living room.

'Hi, Nick! Hello, Briana, nice to see you again! Come in! Want a nightcap? We always have something round about now; I was just on my way to the kitchen. Enjoyed yourself?'

'Hello! Yes, very much. Thanks for putting me up for the night.'

Charlotte nodded. 'No problem. Come and say hello to Ron!'

Briana turned to Nick. She managed to sound quite natural. 'Thanks for inviting me and for the lift.'

His eyes were fixed on Briana's face; his mother thought she saw a fleeting expression that made her start. No . . . that was a stupid idea; Briana would be leaving again soon.

His voice included them both. 'Sleep well!' He gave Briana a last glance. 'Glad you enjoyed yourself; that was my intention!' He turned and the door shut with a click behind him.

A couple of minutes later, after a chat with his parents, she escaped to her room.

Perhaps Li was sharing the night with him. The thought was unbearable. He'd kissed her; but a kiss probably meant nothing to him. Perhaps he felt sorry for her; that idea embarrassed her. Briana knew she wouldn't sleep well tonight.

8

She didn't wait for the lift. Briana raced up the stairwell as if the hounds of hell were at her heels; by the time she reached the third floor she was out of breath.

There was the typical smell of disinfectant in the air; ahead of her the corridor was long and anonymous with a shiny polished floor. Briana spotted Nick's tall figure before he saw her. He was obviously nervous; he was pacing up and down like a tiger in a cage. He had his back towards her at the moment and he was running his hand through his hair impatiently.

She steadied her thoughts and caught her breath. The sounds of her sandals slapping the floor made him turn around quickly. His face was grim, and the closer she got, the better Briana could see his features. They were drawn.

'How is she?' Briana's voice was small and frightened. Fearful images had been growing in her mind all the way to the hospital. Briana still had haunting memories of how her gran had died before she'd been able to get to the hospital. She couldn't bear to think she might lose Phoebe now as well.

'She's holding her own, but the next twenty-four hours will be critical.' His reply was matter-of-fact, but the expression on his face wasn't. He looked strained and tense.

She longed to reach up and touch his cheek, but of course she didn't. She felt relief that Phoebe was still alive, and the nightmare of her gran's death hadn't repeated itself — not so far anyway.

His voice was clipped as he looked at her. 'How did you know she was here?'

Briana's hand went to her throat. 'Phoebe told Joyce where I was, and Joyce phoned your mother. I couldn't believe it when I heard Phoebe was in hospital with a heart attack. I didn't even realise she had heart trouble, did you?'

He shrugged and frowned, his dark eyes level under drawn brows. 'No! If she had problems it's not surprising ... she's nearly eighty, smokes too much, and probably doesn't always look after herself because she's left to her own devices too much. She let slip to me more than once that she'd forgotten to take her medication for high blood-pressure ... so ... !' The lines on his face deepened and Briana felt a flicker of apprehension.

Was it her imagination or was there a suggestion of reproach in his tone? 'Phoebe never mentioned anything about blood pressure, and I never saw her with tablets. She's been tired a lot recently but I couldn't judge what was normal or what was unusual.'

'Tiredness doesn't cause a heart attack.'

Nervously she bit her lip. 'I tried to keep her out of everything concerned with plans for the tourists coming to

146

Turtle because I didn't want to put her under any kind of strain.' Briana was really worried. 'Can . . . can I see her?'

He nodded. There was an edge to his voice and his expression was stern. 'She wants to see you. Intensive Care is at the end of the corridor. Ring for admission. You won't be able to stay for long. She's on a drip, but I think she's beginning to feel better now.'

The words would have calmed her; she couldn't help the exasperation in her voice as she recalled how listless Phoebe had been, and how she'd grumbled more often than usual during the last couple of days. 'Oh . . . Why didn't I ask Mary? I was so tied up in settling the tourists . . . ' She was hoping for some kind of consolation but was disappointed.

He took a firm stance and viewed her with direct, accusing eyes. 'No use crying over spilt milk — but now you mention it, I'm sure this tourist business hasn't done Phoebe any good at all. I warned you weeks ago! In fact I think it's bothered her a lot. Perhaps it'd have been better for Phoebe and everyone else if you'd never come to Turtle Island. Without all the extra fuss, Phoebe wouldn't be in hospital today.' His lips were thin lines and his gaze was angry.

Briana stiffened with shock; the caustic tone of his voice made her flush before she went white like a sheet. She was silenced by his expression. 'Pardon? What did you say?' She couldn't believe he was being so spiteful, with Phoebe lying critically ill in a hospital bed just a few doors away.

His voice was quiet, but it held an undertone of contempt. A cold knot formed in her stomach. 'Before you came here with your hair-brained scheme for island tourism Phoebe was living a quiet, comfortable, if frugal existence. True, she couldn't afford much in the way of luxury, but she managed, and would have gone on managing — she's a strong, independent, fighting character, as you well know. Then you turned up, with ideas and promises.'

'Phoebe probably suspected they might turn her daily routine inside out and it worried her. Knowing how much she was looking forward to your visit, and how much she likes you, I'm sure she didn't protest much, or show you how anxious she was. If you'd had a bit of sense in your head you'd have realised how much it bothered her, and left well alone.'

She flinched and Briana felt ice spreading through her limbs. Her mouth tightened and stiffened as she looked up into his familiar face and then a slight tremor touched her stiff lips. He made her sound like a barging, uncaring, ruthless female. Her breath was shallow and her senses drugged. He was the man she'd coveted all her life and it was unbearable for her to listen with rising dismay to his barbed and hurtful insults.

'You don't expect me to answer, I hope?' She took a deep breath and tried to steady her voice. 'You know that I love Phoebe. I'd do anything . . . anything at all . . . to turn back the clock and make her well, but I can't. I'd never intentionally harm her, and I don't believe that I caused her heart attack, even if you do! Excuse me!' She brushed past him and hoped he didn't see the tears in her eyes.

He lifted his hand in a vague restraining motion and then ran it through his hair instead. He stared down the empty corridor after Briana and looked at the swinging doors. His mouth tightened and his expression darkened before he finally turned away to get out of the antiseptic atmosphere that he hated so much, away from memories that cut him to the core even after all these years.

She waited outside Phoebe's cubicle for a few minutes, leaning her back against a wall. She swallowed hard, couldn't hold back the tears, but after a few minutes she lifted her chin and threw back her head before she pushed open the door to the room where Phoebe was lying. Phoebe smiled as she approached.

Briana bent down and kissed Phoebe's cheek. She gave her a quick hug being careful not to disturb the drip attached to one of Phoebe's arms.

'Save your tears, child! That's enough of that, Briana, I'm not going to die.' Phoebe looked up and gave her a weak smile.

Briana was glad Phoebe had found her own reasons for Briana's red-rimmed eyes. She'd managed to keep herself under control until Nick had set the tears flowing. Briana's voice had a slight hiccup in it. 'Can I have that in writing, please? Ph — Phoebe — I'm so sorry! How do you feel? And why wasn't I there to help?'

'I feel a lot better. As soon as they put me on this drip, the pain disappeared. I feel a bit of a fraud now.'

'How long were you in pain?'

'I didn't notice anything until this morning. I didn't want to make a fuss. I thought it was just indigestion at first, but it got worse, and just before lunch my chest felt like it was being crushed in a vice. Joyce came up to ask you something about the evening meal for the tourists. She called the hospital helicopter straight away, and the rest is history.'

Briana could tell that Phoebe was feeling relatively comfortable and was showing the first tentative signs of her fighting spirit again. It reassured her a little, and she relaxed. 'Don't try to push things. You have to take things easy for a while whether you like it or not — you realise that don't you? Don't try arguing with the nurses or doctors!'

Phoebe gave a gruff laugh. 'I'm trying to be pleasant, and keep my tongue in check. Briana, can you get me my pyjamas and the rest of the stuff I need? I feel awful in this thing.' She tugged at the shoulder of the blue cotton gown with her free hand.

'Of course, but they won't let me in again today, they only gave me ten minutes now — you are supposed to be resting. I'll come tomorrow morning, promise! And I'll bring everything you need with me then.'

Phoebe nodded, and a nurse checking the machinery of the neighbouring patient gave Briana a knowing look.

Briana gave Phoebe another brief kiss. 'Phoebe, I have to go. I'm glad you're feeling more comfortable. I hope that you'll feel even better by tomorrow and perhaps I can stay a bit longer and we can talk then.'

Phoebe stoked Briana's hand. 'I'll try. Sorry to have caused all this trouble, my dear!'

Briana felt the tears welling again. 'Don't be silly, Phoebe! I'm so glad Joyce came at just the right moment. I dread to think what might have happened if you'd been on your own all day. I'll see you tomorrow!'

'Oh . . . Briana before I forget. If something happens to me, you should know that I've left Turtle Island jointly to you and Nick. I fixed things with

Johnson & Baker, a firm of lawyers down by the harbour, years ago. When I first did it, I left it to your gran and Nick because I thought they were the best people to make sure the villagers get a fair deal. I changed it to you and Nick when your gran died.'

Briana's mouth opened in surprise. 'You . . . you did what!'

Phoebe gave a boisterous laugh. 'Briana, close your mouth! It's only an island! I'll see you tomorrow!'

Briana was still shocked, but knew this wasn't the time or the place to bother Phoebe with a conversation that could wait. She smiled back weakly, tried to appear normal, and waved to her. Phoebe lifted her hand and smiled back as the door closed.

Briana walked slowly through the department and out through the swing doors. She couldn't believe what Phoebe had said; but somehow it helped to alleviate the pain of Nick's attack. Even if Nick held her to be responsible for Phoebe's heart attack,

Phoebe loved her enough to entrust her with the care of what she prized most in this life.

The corridor outside was empty, and Briana's thoughts were still whirling. The lift was busy whizzing up and down, so she headed for the stairwell. At the turn of each storey, a window looked out over the entrance area. Glancing down, Briana picked out Nick's red convertible in the parking lot. He was leaning against the bodywork, looking at his watch and waiting.

She wondered if he might be waiting for her. Perhaps he had a bad conscience — but it didn't matter any more. He'd spoken his mind, and she knew where she stood.

Briana went straight down to the village as soon as she landed on Turtle, because she knew that they would all be worried and waiting for news. They were, and all of them gathered quickly when she reached the group of huts. She gave them as much positive news as she could.

Back at the house again, she wasn't hungry although she hadn't eaten anything since breakfast with Charlotte. She spent a couple of restless hours wondering how Phoebe was getting on, and what the situation at the hospital would be like. She tried to avoid thinking about Nick; it hurt too much.

The telephone's shrill tones cut through the silence and Briana's heart started to race. Oh no! Please don't let it be the hospital with bad news! A cold knot formed in her stomach. She moved forward like a machine and picked up the receiver with hands that weren't steady. 'Hello!'

'Briana?'

The sound of his voice was a small shock, but with a jolt of recognition came the relief that Phoebe was probably still OK. He spoke again, 'Briana!'

She gripped the telephone even harder, until the knuckles stood out white on her hand. 'Nick? You . . . you gave me an awful fright, I thought it was the hospital . . . '

'I didn't think about that. Sorry!'

She had a bitter taste in her mouth. 'What can I do for you?'

'I want to talk to you . . . about this afternoon.'

She drew a deep breath and said, 'But I don't want to talk to you about it, Nick! I think it's better if we avoid one another in the future, don't you?'

She heard what sounded like him sucking in air. 'I . . . I can understand how you feel, but . . . '

'Then let's leave it at that. Let's concentrate on Phoebe, and the fact we both want to see her healthy and happy. We don't have to get on with each other to do that.' Briana was finding it harder to ignore what she felt inside; her throat was closing up. 'Goodnight, Nick!' She put down the receiver and felt an awful sense of loss.

She was grateful when the first daylight crept through the shutters, and gave her a plausible reason to get up and do something. She looked in on the tourists, and found they were still enjoying their stay and that they didn't have any problems for her to solve.

She visited Phoebe early in the afternoon with her personal things, and was relieved to find her looking well and that her conversation was as lively as ever. The nursing staff was carefully optimistic when she asked questions.

The following week was strange. Sometimes Briana felt like Alice down the rabbit hole. Phoebe improved and recovered slowly, and that was wonderful after all the worry, but Briana found herself spending lots of time and energy in making sure that she wouldn't bump into Nick on her visits. She visited Phoebe when she thought Nick would be too busy, and she also checked the car park and adjoining road when she arrived, to be certain he wasn't around.

She still felt upset, not just because what he said had hurt and troubled her, but also because her own dreams and hopes had crumbled around her to a pile of rubble.

After a couple of days Phoebe was allowed to leave Intensive Care and she was moved to a private room. Her condition had stabilised. With persuasion, Phoebe had agreed she would spend the first week after she was finally discharged with Mary. She had to come to the hospital for checkups for a couple of days anyway, so it was more sensible to be in easy reach of the hospital.

Briana and Mary had agreed that it'd be better for Phoebe if she came back to Turtle only after the hospital gave the all clear, and when the tourists had disappeared from the island again. At the moment everyone was relieved that Phoebe was fairly sensible, and was agreeing to any plans they made for her. Mary and Briana knew it was because Phoebe would agree to anything if she thought it would help her get out of hospital faster.

When the last visitor left Turtle Island, Briana was somehow glad that the island was back to normal again

— even though the visitors had been no problem, and the scheme had been successful. Some visitors hoped to return next year again.

Briana knew she should leave, but she couldn't until she was sure Phoebe could manage. Her headmaster at home was sympathetic when she phoned, but he warned her that if she wasn't back on time, the education authorities would install a temporary teacher for a term, and she'd have to apply again for another job.

One lovely Sunday afternoon, Briana made her way to Phoebe's room. It was a very peaceful and pleasant place overlooking an inner courtyard. A bougainvillea bush loaded down with bright purple leaves framed the window, and the branches brushed the framework with a scratching sound when the wind got angry.

Nick had arranged for Phoebe to have a private room and, despite the fact that Briana found it difficult to come to terms with what he'd said to her, she was still glad that Phoebe was getting all the care and attention money could buy.

Phoebe patted the seat of the bedside chair with a bony veined hand. She was dressed in lightweight beige slacks and a pale yellow T-shirt. Lying on top of the covers, her head was propped up on a couple of soft pillows, and her hair was tightly plaited as usual. Her bright blue eyes twinkled. 'Sit down, Briana, and tell me about Turtle. Heavens, how I miss it!'

Briana's honey-coloured eyes softened and she laughed gently. 'You've only been away two weeks. Nothing has changed. Everyone sends their love. Look!' She handed Phoebe a beautifully woven palm fan. 'Joyce sent you that, in case it's too warm for you here. She's coming to see you tomorrow.'

Phoebe chuckled and her expression lightened. 'I'll be leaving here in a day or two. I've promised Mary I'll drive her mad for a couple of days, and then I can return to my own bed again. I never thought I would miss it so much — lumps and all!'

Briana nodded knowingly. 'Yes I know — but they'll only let you out if you promise to do as you're told!' She paused. 'I . . . I have to go back to the UK soon, Phoebe, you know that, don't you? But I'll stay as long as I can.'

Phoebe patted her arm. 'I realise that, love. Life goes on. I'll miss you, but you'll come back soon — when you've sorted out your gran's debts, I hope? What about Christmas? This visit hasn't been all I hoped it would be for you. Next time I want you to enjoy yourself properly — no work next time!'

Phoebe noticed the dark shadows under the young woman's eyes, and wondered if it was only her imagination or were Briana's cheekbones more prominent than a couple of weeks ago? The girl spent too much time worrying.

Briana felt tears at the back of her eyes. 'I'll come if I can, of course.' She'd have to find a plausible excuse. She didn't want to meet Nick again.

That chapter was closed, and she didn't intend to open the book ever again.

Phoebe shifted and sat up straight. 'You've only just missed Nick. Half-an-hour ago.'

'Did I?' Briana bent and shifted her shoulder bag around.

If Phoebe noticed that Nick and Briana never visited together, or even at roughly the same time, she didn't say so. She didn't comment on the fact that Briana was deliberately avoiding the subject of Nick either.

'Nick said he's off on a business trip to the States starting tomorrow; for two or three weeks!'

Briana nodded without commenting, and felt relieved. At least she wouldn't have to worry about seeing him again. 'I won't see him before I leave then.'

Phoebe studied the dejected expression in Briana's eyes; however much she was trying to hide it, something was wrong. Phoebe longed to interfere, but knew she would harvest no thanks if she did, so she left well alone.

'Have the tourists left? What did they think of Turtle? Tell me what they said!'

Briana was glad to change the subject; she told Phoebe about how the visitors had departed and how enthusiastic they'd been about everything. Phoebe watched her closely and nodded, but she wasn't listening properly or thinking wholly about Turtle.

Nick was in America; now there was no chance of meeting him unexpectedly. He'd already sent Phoebe a postcard on arrival, and had added a *P.S.*, saying *Best wishes to Briana from me*. He was being polite. She had no urge to read the words for herself. Phoebe moved to Mary's, and the two older women, seemed to be mastering the situation well.

Free to wander after visiting Phoebe, she made her way to the bistro and Gloria greeted her like an old friend. Gloria asked about Phoebe and told Briana. 'I'm going to call at Mary's on my way home tomorrow, to see her.'

Briana smiled up at her. 'I'm sure

she'd love to see you.'

Gloria asked. 'What would you like?'

'A cappuccino, please!'

'Coming up.'

Gloria wove her way with accomplished ease between the tangles of black shiny chairs to the counter. Briana followed her with her eyes, and then caught sight of Nick's mother standing in the doorway. Charlotte Thornton glanced around, and her face brightened when she spotted Briana. She came over.

'Briana, what a nice surprise. Lovely to see you. Are you alone?'

Briana nodded.

'May I join you?'

Briana gestured towards the opposite chair. 'By all means, please do!'

Charlotte made herself comfortable and deposited some packages on one of the empty chairs. She asked about Phoebe. 'I visited her before she moved to Mary's. She looks well, doesn't she? She's raring to get back to Turtle.'

Briana laughed softly. 'Yes, I know.

She doesn't really feel happy anywhere else. Although I think the hospital care and Mary's cooking have also improved her health generally. I think she's put on a little weight! How are you, and Ron? It seems ages since you put me up that night. Our breakfast was the last carefree moment before the storm broke.'

'Ron's fine! As long as he has a plane to maintain and a good meal on the table, he's a fairly contented man.' She gave Briana a motherly smile, and then cleared her throat. 'I'm really glad I've bumped into you like this. Something's been bothering me. My son told me he'd been rude and unkind to you the last time you met.'

The colour flooded and then faded in Briana's face. She looked down but recovered quickly.

Charlotte Thornton didn't miss a thing. 'Nick doesn't usually let me in on the personal side of life, quite rightly of course — he's an adult and capable of making his own decisions. Something must have really troubled him. Would it be too rude of me to ask what was wrong? What exactly did Nick do, or say?'

Briana looked at the older woman and took a deep breath. 'Oh, it was nothing that he hadn't said before, just in different words. It just caught me a bit off-balance because he was so direct when he said it, that's all.'

Charlotte Thornton sighed. 'Oh dear! Nick still exasperates me at times, Briana; but all men are exasperating sometimes, aren't they? It's almost as if they belong to another species! If it isn't anything too personal, would you mind telling me what it was all about? I'd like to help if I can, Ron and I like you, and of course I'm curious.'

Briana answered a question with a question, because her curiosity got the better of her too. 'What exactly did Nick tell you?'

'Nothing much, just that he'd been very unkind to you. I was as surprised to hear even that — he doesn't like admitting he's in the wrong!'

Briana hooked her cup and took a sip. 'In a nutshell, he just said I was probably responsible for Phoebe's heart attack by bringing tourists to Turtle; he thought I'd caused too much stress for Phoebe. He told me he wished I'd never come here.'

Charlotte's voice was a mixture of shock and surprise. 'What? You don't believe that do you? Rubbish! No wonder he feels guilty. I can't believe Nick could be so insensitive.' Charlotte touched Briana's hand briefly. 'Phoebe was always a strong character and she has always made her own decisions. If she didn't like your ideas for Turtle Island, she'd have stopped you straight away. She's not senile. You have no reason to think her heart attack had anything to do with you. What a stupid idea!'

Charlotte shook her head in disbelief. 'Even if that son of mine really believed your idea was wrong, it's not his business. Phoebe is still in charge of her own life. You can get heart attacks for all kinds of reasons. I suspect that even if Phoebe did have something wrong health-wise that led up to the heart attack, she hid it quite successfully from everyone because she didn't want anyone to know, or to fuss. I'm also absolutely sure that she'd have stopped your plans for tourists if she thought it was wrong for her, or for Turtle, even if the reason hurt you in some way!'

Charlotte's words made her feel a little better.

Briana shrugged. 'Thanks! But it doesn't matter any more. I'm leaving soon so Nick and I won't argue, or annoy each other about tourists, or Phoebe anything else more.'

Charlotte Thornton still looked slightly shocked. 'Briana, please don't think too badly of him. I have to explain in his defence, although it is not really an excuse, that Nick has a horror of hospitals, especially anything to do with Intensive Care. When Darren's plane crashed, he was

169

still alive, and they rushed him to hospital. He was unconscious for two days before he died; Nick was with him all the time right up to the end.

'He and Darren were almost like one single entity; he suffered terribly. Hospitals are still his Achilles' heel. It'll take something good, like the birth of a baby, to eradicate the negative memories he has of hospitals.'

Briana flinched at the thought of Nick with a baby of his own. She felt sorry for Charlotte. It must be hard to talk to a comparative stranger about the death of her son. Her voice mirrored her sympathy. 'That must have been a nightmare — for Nick, and for all of the family. How awful to lose someone, after days of hoping things will turn out for the best.'

Charlotte's eyes were bright with moisture. 'Yes, it was a terrible time. Oh dear! Men can be so stupid sometimes. I'm sure he just lashed out at you without thinking — just because you happened to be at the wrong place, at the wrong time. You know how fond Nick is of Phoebe.'

Briana nodded. 'Please don't worry! I know Nick genuinely cares for Phoebe, and I know now that he'll care for her after I've left. When it comes down to it, nothing else is important, is it? Don't let it bother you; they were just words.' Briana wanted to change the subject. She picked up her cup and took another sip. 'Let's talk about something else. How are Sally and the boys? Do you like Brett? He seems to be a nice chap, and Nick said the boys seem to like him.'

Charlotte Thornton took the hint, and they talked quite comfortably about things until Briana finally looked at her watch some time later. Briana got up and offered her hand.

'Goodbye, Charlotte. It was lovely to meet you again before I leave. Thank you for your hospitality, and please remember me to Ron. If you ever come on holiday to the UK, Phoebe has my address, I'd love to see you both.'

Charlotte took her hand and pressed it gently. 'Briana, please don't think badly of Nick, he's not usually pig-headed and offensive. I don't know what got into him. I hope we'll meet again very soon.'

Briana didn't think it was likely, but she smiled back at the older woman anyway without answering.

Next day, before she went to Mary's, she went looking for the firm of lawyers Phoebe had mentioned. The office buildings were old fashioned, the furnishing old and traditional; she was lucky — she was able to talk to the main partner without an appointment. He was kind and understanding; and listened closely to her explanation and request. She left the offices feeling a lot happier even though Mr Johnson had tried to change her mind.

'Miss Norton, the island is probably worth a great deal more than three-quarters of a million dollars on the open market! Please think seriously about what you're doing. You're practically

172

giving it away with very few strings attached.'

Briana nodded. 'I know what I'm doing, Mr Johnson. The island was never mine, so I won't miss it if I don't inherit part of it! If Mr Thornton agrees to be responsible for Phoebe McAllister as long as she lives, I think it's a fair bargain. All I want is that Phoebe has a trouble-free old age. I can't provide her with any financial help, and I'm too far away to help her physically; Mr Thornton can do both. I'm sure he'll make Phoebe's life as pleasant as possible.'

She paused. 'To be honest, I think he'd have done that anyway, even without Turtle Island; he's genuinely fond of Miss McAllister. It's not a spontaneous decision of mine; I've thought about it seriously. I want what's best for Phoebe too. Oh by the way! . . . It might upset her if she knew I'd given Turtle Island away before I'd even inherited it, so I'm depending on your discretion. It might be sensible to tell

Mr Thornton, so he knows where he stands.'

He shook his head. 'I would never abuse a client's confidence without their permission. Ms McAllister would have to agree to let me reveal the contents of her will to Mr Thornton. I'd have to explain why I wanted to inform him — and then she'd find out your part in everything. You just said you didn't want her to be upset.' He paused. 'There's nothing stopping you sending him a copy of the agreement you want us to draw up for you, though. That's up to you. Mr Thornton can draw his own conclusions from the text.

'I'd like to make a suggestion — I think if you are determined to go through with this, you should include some kind of clause that reverses the agreement should Mr Thornton ever abuse the situation . . . if for example he uses the island for any enterprise that is against Ms McAllister's interests. The older she gets, the more she will rely on his decisions, and I don't know the gentleman well enough to judge whether he'll always decide wisely.'

Briana nodded thoughtfully. 'You mean putting in a kind of controlling stipulation. Yes, I suppose you're right — I just want Phoebe to be able to carry on her life as before, but perhaps with less financial worry, until the day she dies.'

He studied her for a moment. 'You're a very unusual young woman. I can't pretend I approve because you may have a reason to look back and regret later, but if you're quite sure?'

Briana nodded. 'Yes, I'm quite, quite sure.' There was no doubt in her voice.

He coughed, and rustled the papers on the desk in front of him. 'Then I'll arrange things.' He looked at his appointment book. 'How about Friday, at three?'

Briana got up, nodded and offered her hand gratefully. Before she left, Briana sent Nick a copy to his office address. She suddenly realised she didn't even know where he lived. It would make Phoebe very curious, if she suddenly asked for Nick's home address. He was still in America, and no-one knew when he was due back.

The day she flew out, she stared down on the green and blue ocean below and even managed to spot the outlines of Turtle before the plane took course for the mainland.

9

It was a dismal evening at the end of October. The evenings were drawing in, and Briana was starting and ending her working day in darkness. Even though it was only a couple of hundred metres from the bus stop in the centre of the village to the cottage, Briana was very glad to reach the low fence that surrounded *Glebe House*.

The wooden gate swung on its rusty hinges and made a faint squeaking sound in the wind. Rainwater was collecting in forlorn puddles on the brickwork pathway leading up to the front door. The rain was cold, and it soaked through the shoulders of her anorak as it plummeted down from the edge of her umbrella. She was frozen and her fingers were numb; she'd been helping to unload indoor plants for the garden centre for the last hour.

If she felt like this now, what would it be like to work in *Plant World* in the depths of winter? She looked around the small garden at the couple of modest trees with their skeletons of remaining foliage; most leaves had already fallen from the trees days ago in a rainbow of red, yellow, rust and gold.

Her teaching job with its related problems seemed like a dream occupation compared to the physical demands of the last couple of weeks in the garden centre. She put on the light and closed the door behind her quickly. She turned up the heating and debated whether it was more important to have a hot bath, or a hot drink. She decided to combine the two, and made herself some hot chocolate.

Briana looked at herself in the mirror. Her hair was untidy — sticking out like a halo around her face. Her features looked haggard, her pale face was free of make-up, and her eyes were too large for her face. Her holiday tan had faded quickly, and her skin looked white and almost translucent.

The reflection showed a cold, tired, hungry female. Briana turned away. A bath, something hot to eat, and an early night would improve her mood immensely. Briana took a sip of the sweet, rich cocoa; it slipped down her throat smoothly. She put the mug on the mantelpiece for a moment and drew the lined curtains. It was comforting to be inside the cottage instead of at the mercy of the wind sweeping through the sheds of the garden centre.

When she returned from the Caribbean she knew that the headmaster couldn't have kept her job open for so long, and she was right. She was forced to take the first offer of work she got, to cover her daily needs — a job in Francis' Garden Centre! Briana was grateful to him for helping her out, even if he couldn't afford to pay her much. It was hard work, but it was better than nothing, and the money covered her daily needs. The fact that she didn't own a car was an obstacle too, but she had no money to buy one. The village didn't have a regular bus service either. Briana hoped she wouldn't be forced into moving away.

She still couldn't believe the house was hers now. Her father had come up trumps and given her a cheque to cover Gran's outstanding debts as well as some money to cover the overheads for a while. She could afford to relax now until she could find another teaching job locally, or some kind of better-paid job.

She arranged the folds of the curtains, while thinking back to when she'd visited Dad and Marcia for the weekend after coming back from Turtle Island. She'd promised to visit them at Gran's funeral, and was glad to have somewhere to go, and something else to think about for a while other than how things were on Turtle Island now, and what Nick was doing, and how much it hurt to know she'd never see him again.

Dad and Marcia made her very welcome, and at some stage she'd mentioned that she was in danger of losing the cottage. She had to explain why. Her father asked, 'How much is involved?'

They'd listened silently and Marcia nodded in silent agreement when her father said, 'We'd like to help, Briana. You've never asked us for anything.' He crossed to the writing desk, took out his chequebook and wrote quickly. Ripping a cheque out of it he came across and handed her the narrow slip of paper. 'No arguments! It's important that you have some kind of security. It's not worth losing that cottage just because you lack a couple of thousand pounds. We want to help Briana, please let us!'

What could she do, but accept the cheque with thanks, and tell them the truth — that they had taken an oppressive weight off her shoulders. She promised to visit them for Christmas, and was grateful for the invitation. It'd be the first Christmas for her on her own, without Gran. It would also be a time of memories and longings for what she'd left behind on Windblown, and on Turtle Island in the Caribbean.

Despite the ache she felt inside for Nick, she reminded herself how much better off she was than a lot of other people. She'd managed to keep Gran's house with Dad's help, she'd a job to keep her fed, and her relationship with her father had improved by leaps and bounds. She no longer felt she was completely alone in the world.

She glanced at Phoebe's latest letter resting on the mantelpiece when she picked up her mug, and vowed to answer it at the weekend. She didn't have to work this Saturday and she was looking forward to lazing through the weekend. An hour later she was warm and glowing, her hair freshly washed and she felt almost human again. She put on her white-towelling dressing-gown, and thrust her feet into the warmest slippers she had. Bliss!

Downstairs again, on her way to the kitchen, and thinking about what she was going to eat, she automatically switched on the TV to listen to the latest news bulletin. Rooting around in the fridge for eggs to make an omelette, the sound of the newsreader's voice was distorted by what sounded like knocking at the door. She grabbed the control on the worktop and hit the mute button. She found the knocking wasn't her imagination; it was real.

It was pitch-dark outside, her nearest neighbour was across a nearby field, and she wasn't expecting visitors. She slipped the safety chain into place before she opened the door and peered through the narrow chink, outside a tall dark silhouette was bending slightly, to fit his head comfortably under the low porch-way.

'Briana? It's me! I've got to talk to you, preferably inside if you don't mind — it rains a lot in this country, doesn't it?'

Briana jumped at the sound of his voice. Was she dreaming, was it an apparition, or just wishful thinking? Her answering voice was a hushed whisper,

'Nick? Is it really you? What on earth are you doing here?'

Her brain began to function again; she searched frantically for a logical explanation for Nick Thornton to be standing on a doorstep in the middle of an English village. Her first instinctive thought was Phoebe and she blustered. 'Is Phoebe ill? Is something wrong?'

His answering words calmed her at once, and although she couldn't see his face clearly, his teeth were strikingly white in the darkness. 'No, absolutely nothing to worry about!'

Briana was still shocked to find him there; she felt almost paralysed. It really was Nick! It was unbelievable. She didn't stop to think that she hadn't seen him face to face since they confronted each other in the hospital corridor; she should have been angry with him, but she found it was impossible to be continually angry with someone you loved so much.

Drops of rain clung to his forehead.

'Briana! Briana . . . I'm getting soaked out here!'

Briana pulled herself together. 'Of course!' She fumbled with the chain. The door opened at last, the chain swung back and forth in an angry motion. The way was free for him; she opened the door and stood aside. 'Come in!'

He didn't need a second invitation, and slid past her through the open doorway. Briana gazed at him, standing there in front of her, brushing the rain from the shoulders of his navy wool coat.

'Whew!' His hands glistened with the rainwater, and he shook them gently.

Briana was too surprised to do more than stare at him; her heart was pounding out of control now she could see his features clearly. She was amazed at the thrill he gave her, despite the fact that she hadn't seen him for a couple of weeks and regardless of the fact they'd parted under a cloud.

She pulled herself together. 'Let me

take your coat.' She reached up and helped him out of it. It bore faint traces of his soap or his aftershave, and she wanted to bury her face in its wetness. Briana went to the kitchen to hang it up behind the door and got him a towel for him to dry his hair.

'That's better!' He peered at her intently and her heart turned over. Handing her the damp towel, he looked around the room, she mused that his head was not far from the low ceiling. 'We have to talk.' Eyeing her carefully, he said. 'Did I get you out of bed?'

Briana was suddenly aware of her dressing-gown. She dropped the towel over the back of a nearby chair, grabbed the edges of the dressing-gown's wide collars and blushed faintly.

'I've . . . I've just had a bath. I was going to get myself something to eat and have an early night.' She started to stutter, and then struggled to sound more conciliatory as she mused that he could interpret her words as a signal she wanted him to keep his visit short.

'Not . . . not that I mean that I'm not glad to see you . . . I just wasn't expecting any visitors.' She was still a little shell-shocked at the sight of Nick Thornton in Gran's kitchen.

'I don't deserve much of a welcome from you, considering how infernally rude I was to you the last time we spoke. I wouldn't have been surprised if you'd slammed the door in my face. You'd have been justified to do so.'

She swallowed hard and tried to think of a clever answer. Nothing came. She gestured towards the couch. 'Won't you sit down? Would you like some tea, coffee, or something stronger?' Her senses were confused, and she fought to appear halfway normal by using hackneyed phrases. 'How's Phoebe? She writes, of course, but it's hard to read between the lines. She seems well, is she?'

'Phoebe? Phoebe's fine. She's ruling the roost on Turtle Island again and despite all the warnings she's smoking cheroots again too. Not as many as before, but she'll never change! I tried to take her to task, she told me in no short terms to mind my own business!'

Briana laughed. She could imagine Phoebe and the situation exactly. Suddenly he reached out and brushed his finger across her cheek. She flinched at his touch, and grew still.

He uttered what sounded almost like a suppressed groan. 'I'm sorry, Briana — for what I said in the hospital. You don't know how much I've regretted it and how ashamed I felt.'

She looked down, but then she raised her eyes to him and waved her hand in a dismissing gesture. 'Let's forget; shall we?'

'No, I can't, and neither can you. I was an idiot, and a bad tempered one into the bargain. I still don't understand what drove me to say those things. I wanted to put things right between us straight away, but I also understood why you were angry and upset, and why you wanted to avoid me.'

She was silent and her eyes were too large in her face. Nick groped around for the right words. He'd stored well-rehearsed phrases in his mind in the hope of convincing her, but seeing her before him emptied his brain of every single one. 'I decided to wait, give you some space, and hoped you'd forgive me later. I forgot all about you needing to fly home and after I got back from the States I was absolutely staggered to find you'd already left.'

She hoped her smile was non-committal. 'It's all water under the bridge now, Nick.' Her voice drifted into a hushed whisper. 'True, I was very angry at the time — but we have to move on. I know now that you honestly care about Phoebe, and your mother put me in the picture about how your brother died in the hospital. That helped me to understand a lot better. Later on I even started to wonder if you might have been right after all; that it was partly my fault.'

His voice was instant and loud. 'No

. . . no of course not! Phoebe's heart attack had nothing to do with you.' He stopped short. 'Why do you hurt the people you love?' He waited patiently, and a pleading wishful smile curved his mouth.

She tried to speak calmly, but her voice wavered . . . he was just speaking in general terms, of course. Briana ploughed on with the conversation and kept things as neutral as she could. 'We all sometimes say things we regret later. You were worried about Phoebe, burdened by memories of your brother's death, and you've always had your doubts about my scheme for friendly tourism on Turtle Island; it all came to the boil at that moment. Let's forget it.' The colour flooded to her cheeks. She tried to force her confused emotions into order; it'd be fatal if he noticed she cared for him as more than a friend. She cleared her throat. 'Are you in the UK on business? How long are you staying?'

He hurried on. 'Business? No, not

business! As soon as I got back from the States, I started to reorganise my schedules in Zenith as fast as I could, so that I could come to the UK. I think people at Zenith are all wondering if I've gone completely mad. And how long I stay depends on you, and what you say!'

'Me? Why me?'

He caught her hands and pulled her closer. His gaze travelled her face and searched her eyes. His brown eyes were liquid pools.

She couldn't think straight, and was just waiting for the inevitable. His mouth covered hers hungrily, and she was shocked at her own eager response.

He held her away from him for a moment and had an almost triumphant expression on his face. 'Wow! They were right!'

Briana mused things had never seemed so confused in her life — what was he talking about now? She didn't really care; she only wanted the feel of his lips on hers again. Her mouth was dry. 'What do you mean? Who are they? And why are you kissing me, when you don't even like me!'

He threw back his head and laughed, but he still held her close in the shelter of his arms. 'They are Phoebe and my mother. They hinted they thought that you liked me, even though I behaved like an idiot in the hospital. That encouraged me to come and find out for myself how you feel.'

'Your mother? Phoebe?' Briana stiffened and tried to push him away, but he held her tight. 'You've been talking about me with other people? Hatching plans, with Phoebe and your mother? How dare you! You came here, just to please them?' She tried to break free.

He imprisoned her hands in his. 'Hey, steady! Calm down! I haven't talked to anyone about us. I haven't talked to anyone about how I feel either; I swear it! Phoebe nearly bit my head off when I told her what I'd said to you at the hospital. Phoebe, and my mother, told me I was a fool to let you go when I clearly cared for you. I don't know how they guessed I was mad about you, but they did. I'd already made my plans to come here; it has absolutely nothing to do with Phoebe or my mother. They don't even know I'm here. I came because I had to. I couldn't go on without seeing you again.'

She took a deep breath. 'Well now you don't need to feel indebted or beholden to me in any way! You've said you're sorry, and that's fine!' Looking flummoxed she managed to continue, 'We don't match at all. We clash all the time; and you don't like me. Don't pretend you do!' She paused. 'Why should the two of them imagine we like each other?'

'Like you? I love you! I never thought I could love someone like I love you. You are more important to me than anything else in my life! I don't care if we clash now and then; it spices up my life. I think we agree about the things that count, don't we?'

His grin was irresistibly devastating. 'Briana, I love you! I don't know how I can carry on living if you send me away; I'd have to live the rest of my life on my own, with dreams of how it could have been.' He looked so serious she couldn't doubt his words. 'You are all I want. Can you find a place in your heart and in your life?'

His words were everything she'd ever dreamed of. Her mouth opened a fraction, but she was lost. 'What about your other girlfriends? What about Li?'

'All gossip and exaggeration, believe me! Li was, and is, a good friend — a business friend. What about your ex-boyfriends? Don't tell me, I don't want to know! I'd only be extremely jealous. What has the past to do with you and me? This is where I hope we'll begin a journey that will last for the rest of our lives.'

His eyes were alight. 'I've been so blind; I thought that I didn't need love in my life, and that I'd never want someone to love me, but I do. I love you more than I could imagine possible, it's been creeping up on me ever since we met, and it really hit me between the eyes when you said it was better for us to avoid each other from then on. I couldn't imagine life without you, and realised how much I needed your approval, your support and your love. I want to take care of you, to be there for you, to share my life with you.'

Some moments later her heart was still hammering foolishly and the pit of her stomach was churning wildly. He stood protectively over her and the smile in his eyes contained a sensuous flame.

Still holding her within the arc of his arm he propelled her to where his coat was hanging. He drew a paper out of the pocket. 'I also want you to be quite sure that I have no ulterior motive for loving you. This is your very honourable, but slightly mad, declaration that you give up your ownership of half of Turtle to me. I have no intention of accepting it.'

He ripped it in pieces and dropped them on the kitchen worktop. 'I have an alternative proposition. How about marrying me, coming back to Windblown, and helping me to keep an eye on Phoebe? Do you love me, can you love me, or not?'

Briana knew he would be a demanding husband, but he would always care for her and she respected him, as well as loved him. 'Of course I love you. That sounds like an interesting, life-consuming deal! What about my plans for friendly tourism on Turtle?'

He groaned. Kissing the bridge of her nose, he said. 'Heavens, what am I getting myself into?'

She buried her head in his chest and they joined together in a peal of laughter.

THE END

We do hope that you have enjoyed reading this large print book.

Did you know that all of our titles are available for purchase?

We publish a wide range of high quality large print books including:
Romances, Mysteries, Classics
General Fiction
Non Fiction and Westerns

Special interest titles available in large print are:
The Little Oxford Dictionary
Music Book, Song Book
Hymn Book, Service Book

Also available from us courtesy of Oxford University Press:
Young Readers' Dictionary
(large print edition)
Young Readers' Thesaurus
(large print edition)

For further information or a free brochure, please contact us at:
Ulverscroft Large Print Books Ltd.,
The Green, Bradgate Road, Anstey,
Leicester, LE7 7FU, England.
Tel: (00 44) **0116 236 4325**
Fax: (00 44) **0116 234 0205**

THE SANCTUARY

Cara Cooper

City lawyer Kimberley is forced to take over an animal sanctuary left to her in a will. The Sanctuary, a Victorian house overlooking the sea, draws Kimberley under its spell. The same cannot be said for her husband Scott, whose dedication to his work threatens their relationship. When Kimberley comes to the aid of handsome, brooding widower Zach Coen and his troubled daughter, she could possibly help them. But will she risk endangering her marriage in the process?

NO MORE ROMANCE

Joan Warde

After the car accident which killed her fiancé and badly injured her, Claire is travelling by train to stay with her, hitherto unknown, Aunt Mary at Forresters Haven. Hoping to avoid the pity she's encountered since the accident, she's infuriated when, on the train, she meets her distant cousin, Adam Forrester, with his patronising manner. However, her Aunt Mary is kind and understanding, there's new interests to occupy her, and there's Timothy . . . but Claire wants no more romance . . .

LOVE ADRIFT

W. S. Foord

In Haven Bay, facing a raging blizzard, lifeboatman Steve Day and his crew pick up survivors from the wrecked Channel Ferry. The blizzard isolates Haven Bay and schoolmistress Helen Foster fears for her boyfriend, a passenger on the ship. Steve Day gives her no time to despair, with a boatload of survivors to look after. But the villagers' concern and help for them is returned by havoc and danger, while Helen discovers an awakening to her way of life.

CLOUDS OVER THE VALLEY

Brenda Castle

Rowan Patrick always believed her mother to have died twenty years ago. Until learning otherwise . . . She goes to the Lake District and finds the Halstead family into which her mother had married after her divorce from Rowan's father. Laura and Chris Halstead are welcoming and explain the calamitous events which severed Rowan's connection with her own mother, twenty years earlier. But Damon Halstead resents Rowan's arrival and suspects her motives in coming . . .

PATHS OF FATE

Sheila Holroyd

When Sara decides to take on a lodger to solve her money worries, her unexpected choice of Walter as a housemate certainly makes life more interesting. But the situation becomes more complicated as her relationship with a charming newcomer at work develops. At the same time, her friend Tabitha is in danger of losing the man she loves. It seems as if their romantic problems can only end in heartbreak . . .